"**Richard Brautigan** is slowly joining Hesse, Golding, Salinger and Vonnegut as a literary magus to the literate young." —*Look* Magazine

"**Brautigan** is, of course, the author of **Trout Fishing in America, A Confederate General from Big Sur,** and **In Watermelon Sugar,** and one of the most authentic spokesmen the Age of Aquarius has yet produced....A gentle and loving book with a curiously innocent approach to life." —*Publishers' Weekly*

His new novel **THE ABORTION** is about "the romantic possibilities of a public library in California."

"**There are,** as one would expect, many delicious moments in the book such as the first time the Librarian and Vida make love....A gentle, funny, beautiful, serious book, and old Brautigan fans will not be disappointed." —College Review Service

"**Bizarre Putdowns**...acute comic observations....Who but Brautigan could divide a seduction into four parts and get away with it? ...A whimsical delight." —*Book World*

"**That a Cult Should Grow Around Brautigan** is no accident....Everything he writes reinforces the modern sense that a literary style might also be a life-style. His writing is as brief and immediate as a telegram or a message left on a door for a friend." —*Saturday Review*

Books by Richard Brautigan

Novels

Trout Fishing in America
A Confederate General from Big Sur
In Watermelon Sugar
The Abortion: An Historical Romance 1966*
The Hawkline Monster: A Gothic Western

Poetry

The Galilee Hitch-Hiker**
Lay the Marble Tea**
The Octopus Frontier**
All Watched Over by Machines of Loving Grace**
Please Plant This Book
The Pill Versus the Springhill Mine Disaster
Rommel Drives On Deep into Egypt

Short Stories

Revenge of the Lawn*

*Published by POCKET BOOKS

**Out of Print

Richard Brautigan

THE Abortion:

An Historical Romance 1966

PUBLISHED BY POCKET BOOKS NEW YORK

THE ABORTION:
An Historical Romance 1966

Simon and Schuster edition published 1971

POCKET BOOK edition published March, 1972

5th printing....................September, 1976

A portion of this book appeared originally in
The Dutton Review, Volume I.

This POCKET BOOK edition includes every word contained in the original, higher-priced edition. It is printed from brand-new plates made from completely reset, clear, easy-to-read type.
POCKET BOOK editions are published by
POCKET BOOKS,
a division of Simon & Schuster, Inc.,
A GULF+WESTERN COMPANY
630 Fifth Avenue,
New York, N.Y. 10020.
Trademarks registered in the United States and other countries.

ISBN: 0-671-80988-1.
Library of Congress Catalog Card Number: 78-150949.
This POCKET BOOK edition is published by arrangement with Simon & Schuster, Inc. Front cover photograph by Edmund Shea.

Printed in the U.S.A.

DEDICATION

Frank:

come on in—
read novel—
it's on table
in front room.
I'll be back
in about
2 hours.

Richard

Contents

BOOK 1:

Buffalo Gals, Won't You Come Out Tonight?

The Library

THIS is a beautiful library, timed perfectly, lush and American. The hour is midnight and the library is deep and carried like a dreaming child into the darkness of these pages. Though the library is "closed" I don't have to go home because this is my home and has been for years, and besides, I have to be here all the time. That's part of my position. I don't want to sound like a petty official, but I am afraid to think what would happen if somebody came and I wasn't here.

I have been sitting at this desk for hours, staring into the darkened shelves of books. I love their presence, the way they honor the wood they rest upon.

I know it's going to rain.

Clouds have been playing with the blue style of the sky all day long, moving their heavy black wardrobes in, but so far nothing rain has happened.

I "closed" the library at nine, but if somebody has a book to bring in, there is a bell they can ring by the door that calls me from whatever I am doing in this place: sleeping, cooking, eating or making love to Vida who will be here shortly.

She gets off work at 11:30.

The bell comes from Fort Worth, Texas. The man

who brought us the bell is dead now and no one learned his name. He brought the bell in and put it down on a table. He seemed embarrassed and left, a stranger, many years ago. It is not a large bell, but it travels intimately along a small silver path that knows the map to our hearing.

Often books are brought in during the late evening and the early morning hours. I have to be here to receive them. That's my job.

I "open" the library at nine o'clock in the morning and "close" the library at nine in the evening, but I am here twenty-four hours a day, seven days a week to receive the books.

An old woman brought in a book a couple of days ago at three o'clock in the morning. I heard the bell ringing inside my sleep like a small highway being poured from a great distance into my ear.

It woke up Vida, too.

"What is it?" she said.

"It's the bell," I said.

"No, it's a book," she said.

I told her to stay there in bed, to go back to sleep, that I would take care of it. I got up and dressed myself in the proper attitude for welcoming a new book into the library.

My clothes are not expensive but they are friendly and neat and my human presence is welcoming. People feel better when they look at me.

Vida had gone back to sleep. She looked nice with her long black hair spread out like a fan of dark lakes upon the pillow. I could not resist lifting up the covers to stare at her long sleeping form.

A fragrant odor rose like a garden in the air above the incredibly strange thing that was her body, motionless and dramatic lying there.

I went out and turned on the lights in the library. It looked quite cheerful, even though it was three o'clock in the morning.

The old woman waited behind the heavy glass of the front door. Because the library is very old-fashioned, the door has a religious affection to it.

The woman had a look of great excitement. She was very old, eighty I'd say, and wore the type of clothing that associates itself with the poor.

But no matter . . . rich or poor . . . the service is the same and could never be any different.

"I just finished it," she said through the heavy glass before I could open the door. Her voice, though slowed down a great deal by the glass, was bursting with joy, imagination and almost a kind of youth.

"I'm glad," I said back through the door. I hadn't quite gotten it open yet. We were sharing the same excitement through the glass.

"It's done!" she said, coming into the library, accompanied by an eighty-year-old lady.

"Congratulations," I said. "It's so wonderful to write a book."

"I walked all the way here," she said. "I started at midnight. I would have gotten here sooner if I weren't so old."

"Where do you live?" I said.

"The Kit Carson Hotel," she said. "And I've written a book." Then she handed it proudly to me as if it were the most precious thing in the world. And it was.

It was a loose-leaf notebook of the type that you find everywhere in America. There is no place that does not have them.

There was a heavy label pasted on the cover and written in broad green crayon across the label was the title:

GROWING FLOWERS BY CANDLELIGHT
IN HOTEL ROOMS
BY
MRS. CHARLES FINE ADAMS

"What a wonderful title," I said. "I don't think we have a book like this in the entire library. This is a first."

She had a big smile on her face which had turned old about forty years ago, eroded by the gases and exiles of youth.

"It has taken me five years to write this book," she said. "I live at the Kit Carson Hotel and I've raised many flowers there in my room. My room doesn't have any windows, so I have to use candles. They work the best.

"I've also raised flowers by lanternlight and magnifying glass, but they don't seem to do well, especially tulips and lilies of the valley.

"I've even tried raising flowers by flashlight, but that was very disappointing. I used three or four flashlights on some marigolds, but they didn't amount to much.

"Candles work the best. Flowers seem to like the smell of burning wax, if you know what I mean. Just show a flower a candle and it starts growing."

I looked through the book. That's one of the things I get to do here. Actually, I'm the only person who gets to do it. The book was written in longhand with red, green and blue crayons. There were drawings of her hotel room with the flowers growing in the room.

Her room was very small and there were many flowers in it. The flowers were in tin cans and bottles and jars and they were all surrounded by burning candles.

Her room looked like a cathedral.

There was also a drawing of the former manager of the hotel and a drawing of the hotel elevator. The elevator looked like a very depressing place.

In her drawing of the hotel manager, he appeared to be very unhappy, tired and looked as if he needed a vacation. He also seemed to be looking over his shoulder at something that was about to enter his vision. It was a thing he did not want to see and it was just about there. Under the drawing was written this:

MANAGER OF THE KIT CARSON HOTEL
UNTIL HE GOT FIRED
FOR DRINKING IN THE ELEVATOR
AND FOR STEALING SHEETS

The book was about forty pages long. It looked quite interesting and would be a welcomed addition to our collection.

"You're probably very tired," I said. "Why don't you sit down and I'll make you a cup of instant coffee?"

"That would be wonderful," she said. "It took me five years to write this book about flowers. I've worked very hard on it. I love flowers. Too bad my room doesn't have any windows, but I've done the best I can with candles. Tulips do all right."

Vida was sound asleep when I went back to my room. I turned on the light and it woke her up. She was blinking and her face had that soft marble quality to it that beautiful women have when they are suddenly awakened and are not quite ready for it yet.

"What's happening?" she said. "It's another book," she replied, answering her own question.

"Yes," I said.

"What's it about?" she said automatically like a gentle human phonograph.

"It's about growing flowers in hotel rooms."

I put the water on for the coffee and sat down beside Vida who curled over and put her head on my lap, so that my lap was entirely enveloped in her watery black hair.

I could see one of her breasts. It was fantastic!

"Now what's this about growing flowers in hotel rooms?" Vida said. "It couldn't be that easy. What's the real story?"

"By candlelight," I said.

"Uh-huh," Vida said. Even though I couldn't see her face, I knew she was smiling. She has funny ideas about the library.

"It's by an old woman," I said. "She loves flowers but she doesn't have any windows in her hotel room, so she grows them by candlelight."

"Oh, baby," Vida said, in that tone of voice she always uses for the library. She thinks this place is creepy and she doesn't care for it very much.

I didn't answer her. The coffee water was done and I took a spoonful of instant coffee and put it out in a cup.

"Instant coffee?" Vida said.

"Yes," I said. "I'm making it for the woman who just brought the book in. She's very old and she's walked a great distance to get here. I think she needs a cup of instant coffee."

"It sounds like she does. Perhaps even a little amyl nitrate for a chaser. I'm just kidding. Do you need any help? I'll get up."

"No, honey," I said. "I can take care of it. Did we eat all those cookies you baked?"

"No," she said. "The cookies are over there in that sack." She pointed toward the white paper bag on the table. "I think there are a couple of chocolate cookies left."

"What did you put them in the sack for?" I said.

"I don't know," she said. "Why does anyone put cookies in a sack? I just did."

Vida was resting her head on her elbow and watching me. She was unbelievable: her face, her eyes, her . . .

"Strong point," I said.

"Am I right?" she said, sleepily.

"Yup," I said.

I took the cup of coffee and put it on a small wooden tray, along with some canned milk and some sugar and a little plate for the cookies.

Vida had given me the tray as a present. She bought it at Cost Plus Imports and surprised me with it one day. I like surprises.

"See you later," I said. "Go back to sleep."

"OK," and pulled the covers up over her head. Farewell, my lovely.

I took the coffee and cookies out to the old woman. She was sitting at a table with her face resting on her elbow and she was half asleep. There was an expression of dreaming on her face.

I hated to interrupt her. I know how much a dream can be worth, but, alas . . . "Hello," I said.

"Oh, hello," she said, breaking the dream cleanly.

"It's time for some coffee," I said.

"Oh, how nice," she said. "It's just what I need to wake me up. I'm a little tired because I walked so far. I guess I could have waited until tomorrow and taken the bus here, but I wanted to bring the book out right away because I just finished it at midnight and I've been working on it for five years.

"Five Years," she repeated, as if it were the name of a country where she was the President and the flowers growing by candlelight in her hotel room were her cabinet and I was the Secretary of Libraries.

"I think I'll register the book now," I said.

"That sounds wonderful," she said. "These are delicious cookies. Did you bake them yourself?"

I thought that was a rather strange question for her to ask me. I have never been asked that question before. It startled me. It's funny how people can catch you off guard with a question about cookies.

"No," I said. "I didn't bake these cookies. A friend did."

"Well, whoever baked them knows how to bake cookies. The chocolate tastes wonderful. So chocolatey."

"Good," I said.

Now it was time to register the book. We register all the books we receive here in our Library Contents Ledger. It is a record of all the books we get day by day, week by week, month by month, year by year. They all go into the Ledger.

We don't use the Dewey decimal classification or any index system to keep track of our books. We record their entrance into the library in the Library Contents Ledger and then we give the book back to its author who is free to place it anywhere he wants in the library, on whatever shelf catches his fancy.

It doesn't make any difference where a book is placed because nobody ever checks them out and nobody ever comes here to read them. This is not that kind of library. This is another kind of library.

"I just love these cookies," the old woman said, finishing the last cookie. "Such a good chocolate flavor. You can't buy these in a store. Did a friend bake them?"

"Yes," I said. "A very good friend."

"Well, good for them. There isn't enough of that thing going on now, if you know what I mean."

"Yes," I said. "Chocolate cookies are good."

Vida baked them.

By now the old woman had finished the last drops of coffee in her cup, but she drank them again, even though they were gone. She wanted to make sure that she did not leave a drop in the cup, even to the point of drinking the last drop of coffee twice.

I could tell that she was preparing to say good-bye because she was trying to rise from her chair. I knew that she would never return again. This would be her only visit to the library.

"It's been so wonderful writing a book," she said. "Now it's done and I can return to my hotel room and my flowers. I'm very tired."

"Your book," I said, handing it to her. "You are free to put it anywhere you want to in the library, on any shelf you want."

"How exciting," she said.

She took her book very slowly over to a section where a lot of children are guided by a subconscious track of some kind to place their books on that shelf.

I don't remember ever seeing anyone over fifty put a book there before, but she went right there as if guided by the hands of the children and placed her book about growing flowers by candlelight in hotel rooms in between a book about Indians (pro) and an illustrated, highly favorable tract on strawberry jam.

She was very happy as she left the library to walk very slowly back to her room in the Kit Carson Hotel and the flowers that waited for her there.

I turned out the lights in the library and took the tray back to my room. I knew the library so well that I could do it in the dark. The returning path to my room was made comfortable by thoughts of flowers, America and Vida sleeping like a photograph here in the library.

The Automobile Accident

THIS library came into being because of an overwhelming need and desire for such a place. There just simply had to be a library like this. That desire brought into existence this library building which isn't very large and its permanent staffing which happens to be myself at the present time.

The library is old in the San Francisco post-earthquake yellow-brick style and is located at 3150 Sacramento Street, San Francisco, California 94115, though no books are ever accepted by mail. They must be brought in person. That is one of the foundations of this library.

Many people have worked here before me. This

place has a fairly rapid turnover. I believe I am the 35th or 36th librarian. I got the job because I was the only person who could fulfill the requirements and I was available.

I am thirty-one years old and never had any formal library training. I have had a different kind of training which is quite compatible with the running of this library. I have an understanding of people and I love what I am doing.

I believe I am the only person in America who can perform this job right now and that's what I'm doing. After I am through with my job here, I'll find something else to do. I think the future has quite a lot in store for me.

The librarian before me was here for three years and finally had to quit because he was afraid of children. He thought they were up to something. He is now living in an old folks' home. I got a postcard from him last month. It was unintelligible.

The librarian before him was a young man who took a six-months leave of absence from his motorcycle gang to put in his tenure here. Afterward he returned to his gang and never told them where he had been.

"Where have you been the last six months?" they asked him.

"I've been taking care of my mother," he said. "She was sick and needed lots of hot chicken soup. Any more questions?" There were no more questions.

The librarian before him was here for two years, then moved suddenly to the Australian bush. Nothing has been heard from him since. I've heard rumors that he's alive, but I've also heard rumors that he's dead, but whatever he's doing, dead or alive, I'm certain he's still in the Australian bush because he said he wasn't coming back and if he ever saw another book again, he'd cut his throat.

The librarian before him was a young lady who quit because she was pregnant. One day she caught the glint in a young poet's eye. They are now living together in the Mission District and are no longer young. She has a beautiful daughter, though, and he's on unemployment. They want to move to Mexico.

I believe it's a mistake on their part. I have seen too many couples who went to Mexico and then immediately broke up when they returned to America. I believe if they want to stay together they shouldn't go to Mexico.

The librarian before her was here for one year. He was killed in an automobile accident. An automobile went out of control and crashed into the library. Somehow it killed him. I have never been able to figure this out because the library is made of bricks.

The 23

Ah, it feels so good to sit here in the darkness of these books. I'm not tired. This has been an average evening for books being brought in: with 23 finding their welcomed ways onto our shelves.

I wrote their titles and authors and a little about the receiving of each book down in the Library Contents Ledger. I think the first book came in around 6:30.

MY TRIKE by Chuck. The author was five years old and had a face that looked as if it had been struck by a tornado of freckles. There was no title on the book and no words inside, just pictures.

"What's the name of your book?" I said.

The little boy opened the book and showed me the drawing of a tricycle. It looked more like a giraffe standing upside down in an elevator.

"That's my trike," he said.

"Beautiful," I said. "And what's your name?"

"That's my trike."

"Yes," I said. "Very nice, but what's your name?"

"Chuck."

He reached the book up onto the desk and then

headed for the door, saying, "I have to go now. My mother's outside with my sister."

I was going to tell him that he could put the book on any shelf he wanted to, but then he was gone in his small way.

LEATHER CLOTHES AND THE HISTORY OF MAN by S. M. Justice. The author was quite motorcyclish and wearing an awful lot of leather clothes. His book was made entirely of leather. Somehow the book was printed. I had never seen a 290-page book printed on leather before.

When the author turned the book over to the library, he said, "I like a man who likes leather."

LOVE ALWAYS BEAUTIFUL by Charles Green. The author was about fifty years old and said he had been trying to find a publisher for his book since he was seventeen years old when he wrote the book.

"This book has set the world's record for rejections," he said. "It has been rejected 459 times and now I am an old man."

THE STEREO AND GOD by the Reverend Lincoln Lincoln. The author said that God was keeping his eye on our stereophonic phonographs. I don't know what he meant by that but he slammed the book down very hard on the desk.

PANCAKE PRETTY by Barbara Jones. The

author was seven years old and wearing a pretty white dress.

"This book is about a pancake," she said.

SAM SAM SAM by Patricia Evens Summers. "It's a book of literary essays," she said. "I've always admired Alfred Kazin and Edmund Wilson, especially Wilson's theories on *The Turn of the Screw.*" She was a woman in her late fifties who looked a great deal like Edmund Wilson.

A HISTORY OF NEBRASKA by Clinton York. The author was a gentleman about forty-seven who said he had never been to Nebraska but he had always been interested in the state.

"Ever since I was a child it's been Nebraska for me. Other kids listened to the radio or raved on about their bicycles. I read everything I could find on Nebraska. I don't know what got me started on the thing. But, any way, this is the most complete history ever written about Nebraska."

The book was in seven volumes and he had them in a shopping bag when he came into the library.

HE KISSED ALL NIGHT by Susan Margar. The author was a very plain middle-aged woman who looked as if she had never been kissed. You had to look twice to see if she had any lips on her face. It was a surprise to find her mouth almost totally hidden beneath her nose.

"It's about kissing," she said.

I guess she was too old for any subterfuge now.

MOOSE by Richard Brautigan. The author was tall and blond and had a long yellow mustache that gave him an anachronistic appearance. He looked as if he would be more at home in another era.

This was the third or fourth book he had brought to the library. Every time he brought in a new book he looked a little older, a little more tired. He looked quite young when he brought in his first book. I can't remember the title of it, but it seems to me the book had something to do with America.

"What's this one about?" I asked, because he looked as if he wanted me to ask him something.

"Just another book," he said.

I guess I was wrong about him wanting me to ask him something.

IT'S THE QUEEN OF DARKNESS, PAL by Rod Keen. The author was wearing overalls and had on a pair of rubber boots.

"I work in the city sewers," he said, handing the book to me. "It's science-fiction."

YOUR CLOTHES ARE DEAD by Les Steinman. The author looked like an ancient Jewish tailor. He was very old and looked as if he had made some shirts for Don Quixote.

"They are, you know," he said, showing the book to me as if it were a piece of cloth, a leg from a pair of trousers.

JACK, THE STORY OF A CAT by Hilda Simpson. The author was a girl about twelve years old, just entering into puberty. She had lemon-sized breasts against a green sweater. She was awakening to adolescence in a delightful way.

"What do you have with you this evening?" I said.

Hilda had brought in five or six books previously.

"It's a book about my cat Jack. He's really a noble animal. I thought I would put him down in a book, bring it here and make him famous," she said, smiling.

THE CULINARY DOSTOEVSKI by James Fallon. The author said the book was a cookbook of recipes he had found in Dostoevski's novels.

"Some of them are very good," he said. "I've eaten everything Dostoevski ever cooked."

MY DOG by Bill Lewis. The author was seven years old and said thank you when he put his book on a shelf.

HOMBRE by Canton Lee. The author was a Chinese gentleman about seventy.

"It's a Western," he said. "About a horse thief. Reading Westerns is my hobby, so I decided to write one myself. Why not? I spent thirty years cooking in a restaurant in Phoenix."

VIETNAM VICTORY by Edward Fox. The author was a very serious young man who said that victory could only be achieved in Vietnam by killing everybody there. He recommended that after we had killed everybody there we turn the country over to

Chiang Kai-shek, so he could attack Red China, then.

"It's only a matter of time," he said.

PRINTER'S INK by Fred Sinkus. The author was a former journalist whose book was almost illegibly written in longhand with his words wrapped around whiskey.

"That's it," he said, handing the book to me. "Twenty years." He left the library unevenly, barely under his own power.

I stood there looking down at twenty years in my hands.

BACON DEATH by Marsha Paterson. The author was a totally nondescript young woman except for a look of anguish on her face. She handed me this fantastically greasy book and fled the library in terror. The book actually looked like a pound of bacon. I was going to open it and see what it was about, but I changed my mind. I didn't know whether to fry the book or put it on the shelf.

Being a librarian here is sometimes a challenge.

UFO VERSUS CBS by Susan DeWitt. The author was an old woman who told me that her book, which was written in Santa Barbara at her sister's house, was about a Martian conspiracy to take over the Columbia Broadcasting System.

"It's all here in my book," she said. "Remember all those flying saucers last summer?"

"I think so," I said.

"They're all in here," she said. The book looked quite handsome and I'm certain they were all in there.

THE EGG LAYED TWICE by Beatrice Quinn Porter. The author said this collection of poetry summed up the wisdom she had found while living twenty-six years on a chicken ranch in San Jose.

"It may not be poetry," she said. "I never went to college, but it's sure as hell about chickens."

BREAKFAST FIRST by Samuel Humber. The author said that breakfast was an absolute requisite for travelling and was overlooked in too many travel books, so he decided that he would write a book about how important breakfast was in travelling.

THE QUICK FOREST by Thomas Funnell. The author was about thirty years old and looked scientific. His hair was thinning and he seemed eager to talk about the book.

"This forest is quicker than an ordinary forest," he said.

"How long did it take you to write it?" I said, knowing that authors seem to like that question.

"I didn't write it," he said. "I stole it from my mother. Serves her right, too. The God-damn bitch."

THE NEED FOR LEGALIZED ABORTION by Doctor O. The author was doctory and very nervous in his late 30s. The book had no title on the cover. The contents were very neatly typed, about 300 pages long.

"It's all I can do," he said.

"Do you want to put it on a shelf yourself?" I said.

"No," he said. "You take care of that yourself. There's nothing else that I can do. It's all a God-damn shame."

It has just started to rain now outside the library. I can hear it splash against the windows and echo among the books. They seem to know it's raining here in the beautiful darkness of lives as I wait for Vida.

Buffalo Gals, Won't You Come Out Tonight?

I MUST tell you right now that most of the library isn't here. This building is not large and couldn't begin to hold all the books that have been brought in over the years.

The library was in existence before it came to San Francisco in the late 1870s, and the library didn't lose a book during the earthquake and fire of 1906. While everybody else was running around like a bunch of chickens with their heads cut off, we were careful: no panic.

This library rests upon a sloping lot that runs all the way through the block down from Clay to Sacramento Street. We use just a small portion of the lot and the rest of it is overgrown with tall grass and bushes and flowers and wine bottles and lovers' trysts.

There are some old cement stairs that pour through green and busy establishments down from the Clay Street side and there are ancient electric lamps, friends of Thomas Edison, mounted on tall metal asparagus stalks.

They are on what was once the second landing of the stairs. The lights don't work any more and everything is so overgrown that it's hard to tell why anything ever existed in the first place.

The back of the library lies almost disappearing in green at the bottom of the stairs.

The front lawn is neat, though. We don't want this place to look totally like a jungle. It might frighten people away.

A little Negro boy comes and mows the lawn every month or so. I don't have any money to pay him but he doesn't mind. He does it because he likes me and he knows that I have to stay inside here, that I can't mow the lawn myself. I always have to be in here ready to welcome a new book.

Right now the lawn has many dandelions on it and thousands of daisies sprawled here and there together like a Rorschach dress pattern designed by Rudi Gernreich.

The dandelions are loners and pretty much stay

off by themselves, but those daisies! I know all this by looking out the heavy glass door.

This place is constantly bathed in the intermediate barking of dogs from early in the morning when the dogs wake up and continuing until late at night when the dogs go to sleep and sometimes they bark in between.

We are just a few doors down from a pet hospital and, though I can't see the hospital, I am seldom without the barking of dogs and I have grown used to it.

At first I hated their damn barking. It had always been a thing with me: a dislike for dogs. But now in my third year here, I've grown accustomed to their barking and it doesn't bother me any more. Actually, I like it sometimes.

There are high arched windows here in the library above the bookshelves and there are two green trees towering into the windows and they spread their branches like paste against the glass.

I love those trees.

Through the glass door and across the street is a big white garage with cars coming and going all the time in hours of sickness and need. There is a big word in blue on the front of the garage: GULF.

Before the library came to San Francisco, it was in Saint Louis for a while, then in New York for a long time. There are a lot of Dutch books somewhere.

Because this building is so small, we have been forced to store thousands of books at another place. We moved into this little brick building after the

'06 business to be on the safe side, but there just isn't enough room here.

There are so many books being written that end up here, either by design or destiny. We have accepted 114 books on the Model T Ford, fifty-eight books on the history of the banjo and nineteen books on buffalo-skinning since the beginning of this library.

We keep all the ledgers here that we use to record the acceptance of each book in, but most of the books themselves are in hermetically-sealed caves in Northern California.

I have nothing to do with the storing of the books in the caves. That's Foster's job. He also brings me my food because I can't leave the library. Foster hasn't been around for a few months, so I guess he's off on another drunk.

Foster loves to drink and it's always easy for him to find somebody to drink with. Foster is about forty years old and always wears a T-shirt, no matter what the weather is about, rain or shine, hot or cold, it's all the same to his T-shirt because his T-shirt is an eternal garment that only death will rob from his body.

Foster has long buffalo-heavy blond hair and I have never seen Foster when he wasn't sweating. He's very friendly in an overweight sort of style, jolly you might say, and has a way of charming people, total strangers, into buying him drinks. He goes off on month-long drunks in the logging towns near the caves, raises hell with the loggers and chases the Indian girls through the woods.

I imagine he'll be down here one of these days, red-faced and hung-over, full of excuses and driving his big green van and all ready to fill it up with another load of books for the caves.

BOOK 2:

Vida

Vida

WHEN I first met Vida she had been born inside the wrong body and was barely able to look at people, wanting to crawl off and hide from the thing that she was contained within.

This was late last year in San Francisco.

She came to the library one evening after she got off work. The library was "closed" and I was in my room making some coffee and thinking about the books that had come into the library that day.

One of the books was about a great octopus that had leather wings and flew through abandoned school yards at night, demanding entrance into the class-rooms.

I was putting some sugar into my coffee when I heard the bell ring ever so slightly, but always just enough to alert me and to summon me.

I went out and turned on the light in the library and there was a young girl at the door, waiting behind the heavy religious glass.

She startled me.

Besides having an incredibly delicate face, beautiful, with long black hair that hung about her shoulders like bat lightning, there was something very unusual about her, but I could not quite tell what that thing was because her face was like a perfect labyrinth that led me momentarily away from a very disturbing thing.

She did not look directly at me as she waited for me to unlock the door and let her in. She was holding something under her arm. It was in a brown paper bag and looked like a book.

Another one for the caves.

"Hello," I said. "Please come in."

"Thank you," she said, coming very awkwardly into the library. I was surprised that she was so awkward. She did not look directly at me and she did not look at the library either. She seemed to be looking at something else. The thing that she was looking at was not in front of me nor behind me nor at the side of me.

"What do you have there? A book?" I said, wanting to sound like a pleasant librarian and make her feel at ease.

Her face was so delicate: the mouth, the eyes, the nose, the chin, the curve of her cheeks all beautiful. She was almost painful to gaze upon.

"Yes," she said. "I hope I didn't disturb you. It's late."

"No," I said. "Not at all. No. Please come over here to the desk and we'll register your book in the Library Contents Ledger. That's how we do it here."

"I was wondering how you were going to do it," she said.

"Did you come far?" I said.

"No," she said. "I just got off work."

She wasn't looking at herself either. I do not know

what she was looking at, but she was looking at something very intently. I believe the thing that she was looking at was inside of herself. It had a shape that only she could see.

She moved very awkwardly over to the desk, stunningly awkward, but again the almost tide-pool delicacy of her face led me away from the source of her awkwardness.

"I hope I'm not disturbing you. I know it's late," she said, kind of hopelessly, and then broke away from the thing that she was looking at, to glance lightspeed at me.

She *was* disturbing me, but not in the way she thought. There was a dynamically incongruous thing about her, but I still couldn't find it. Her face, like a circle of mirrors, led me away from it.

"No, not at all," I said. "This is my job and I love doing it. There's no place I would rather be than where I am now."

"What?" she said.

"I love my work," I said.

"It's good you're happy," she said. She said the word happy as if she were looking at it from a great distance through a telescope. The word sounded celestial upon her mouth, stark and Galilean.

Then I noticed what was so extraordinarily strange about her. Her face was so delicate, perfect, but her body was fantastically developed for the fragility of her face.

She had very large fully realized breasts and an incredibly tiny waist and large full hips that tapered down into long majestic legs.

Her body was very sensual, inciting one to think of lust, while her face was Botticellian and set your mind to voyaging upon the ethereal.

Suddenly she sensed my recognition of her body. She blushed bitterly and reached into the paper bag and took out her book.

"This is my book," she said.

She put it down on the desk and almost stepped back when she did it. She was going to step back but then she changed her mind. She glanced at me again and I could feel somebody inside of her looking out as if her body were a castle and a princess lived inside.

The book had a plain brown wrapper on it and there was no title. The book looked like a stark piece of ground burning with frozen heat.

"What's it about?" I said, holding the book in my hand, feeling almost a hatred coming from within the book.

"It's about this," she said and suddenly, almost hysterically, she unbuttoned her coat and flung it open as if it were a door to some horrible dungeon filled with torture instruments, pain and dynamic confession.

She was wearing a blue sweater and skirt and a pair of black leather boots in the style of this time. She had a fantastically full and developed body under her clothes that would have made the movie stars and beauty queens and showgirls bitterly ooze dead make-up in envy.

She was developed to the most extreme of Western man's desire in this century for women to look:

the large breasts, the tiny waist, the large hips, the long *Playboy* furniture legs.

She was so beautiful that the advertising people would have made her into a national park if they would have gotten their hands on her.

Then her blue eyes swirled like a tide pool and she started crying.

"This book is about my body," she said. "I hate it. It's too big for me. It's somebody else's body. It's not mine."

I reached into my pocket and took out a handkerchief and a candy bar. When people are troubled or worried, I always tell them that it will be all right and give them a candy bar. It surprises them and it's good for them.

"Everything's going to be all right," I said.

I gave her a Milky Way. She held it in her startled hand, staring at it. And I gave her the handkerchief.

"Wipe your eyes," I said. "And eat the candy bar while I get you a glass of sherry."

She fumbled abstractedly with the candy bar wrapper as if it were a tool from a distant and future century while I went and got some sherry for us. I figured that we would both need it.

When I came back she was eating the candy bar. "Now isn't that good," I said, smiling.

The ludicrousness of me giving her a candy bar made her smile, ever so slightly, and almost look directly at me.

"Please sit down over here," I said, motioning toward a table and some chairs. She sat down as if her body were six inches larger than she was. After she had sat down, her body was still sitting down.

I poured us each a glass of Gallo sherry, all the library could afford, and then there was a kind of awkward silence as we sat there sipping our sherry.

I was going to tell her that she was a beautiful girl and she shouldn't feel bad about it, that she was all wrong in denouncing herself, but then I changed my mind instantly.

That was not what she wanted to hear and that wasn't really what I wanted to say. After all, I have a little more sense than that. We both didn't want to hear what I first thought of telling her.

"What's your name?" I said.

"Vida. Vida Kramar."

"Do you like to be called V-(ee)-da or V-(eye)-da?"

That made her smile.

"V-(eye)-da."

"How old are you?"

"Nineteen. Soon I'll be twenty. On the tenth."

"Do you go to school?"

"No, I work at night. I went to State for a while, then UC, but I don't know. Now I'm working at night. It's OK."

She was almost looking at me.

"Did you just finish your book?" I said.

"Yes, I finished it yesterday. I wanted to tell how it is to be like me. I figured it was the only thing left for me to do. When I was eleven years old, I had a thirty-six-inch bust. I was in the sixth grade.

"For the last eight years I've been the object,

veneration and butt of at least a million dirty jokes. In the seventh grade they called me 'points.' Isn't that cute? It never got any better.

"My book is about my body, about how horrible it is to have people creeping, crawling, sucking at something I am not. My older sister looks the way I really am.

"It's horrible.

"For years I had a recurrent dream that I got up in the middle of the night and went into my sister's bedroom and changed bodies with her. I took off my body and put on her body. It fit perfectly.

"When I woke up in the morning, I had on my own true body and she had this terrible thing I'm wearing now. I know it's not a nice dream, but I had it all during my early teens.

"You'll never know how it is to be like I am. I can't go anywhere without promoting whistles, grunts, howls, minor and major obscenities and every man I meet wants to go to bed instantly with me. I have the wrong body."

She was staring directly at me now. Her vision was unbroken and constant as a building with many windows standing fully here in this world.

She continued: "My whole life has just been one torment. I, I don't know. I wrote this book to tell how horrible physical beauty is, the full terror of it.

"Three years ago a man was killed in an automobile accident because of my body. I was walking along a highway. I had gone to the beach with my family, but I couldn't stand it any longer.

"They demanded that I put on a bathing suit. 'Don't be bashful, just relax and enjoy yourself.' I was miserable with all the attention I was getting. When an eighty-year-old man dropped his ice-cream cone on his foot, I put my clothes back on and went for a walk along the highway up from the beach. I had to go somewhere.

"A man came driving by in his car. He slowed down and was gawking at me. I tried to ignore him but he was very persistent. He forgot all about where he was and what he was doing and drove his car right into a train.

"I ran over and he was still alive. He died in my arms, still staring at me. It was horrible. There was blood all over both of us and he wouldn't take his eyes off me. Part of the bone was sticking out of his arm. His back felt funny. When he died, he said, 'You're beautiful.' That's just what I needed to make me feel perfect forever.

"When I was fifteen a student in a high-school chemistry class drank hydrochloric acid because I wouldn't go out with him. He was a little crazy, anyway, but that didn't make me feel any better. The principal prohibited me from wearing a sweater to school.

"It's this," Vida said, gesturing rain-like toward her body. "It's not me. I can't be responsible for what it does. I don't attempt to use my body to get anything from anyone and I never have.

"I spend all my time hiding from it. Can you imagine spending your whole life hiding from your own body as if it were a monster in a Grade B movie, but still every day having to use it to eat, sleep and get from one place to another?

"Whenever I take a bath I always feel as if I'm going to vomit. I'm in the wrong skin."

All the time she told me these things she did not take her eyes off me. I felt like a statue in a park. I poured her another glass of sherry and one for myself. I had a feeling that we were going to need a lot of sherry before the night was over.

"I don't know what to say," I said. "I'm just a librarian. I can't pretend that you are not beautiful. That would be like pretending that you are someplace else in the world, say China or Africa, or that you are some other kind of matter, a plant or a tire or some frozen peas or a bus transfer. Do you understand?"

"I don't know," she said.

"It's the truth. You're a very pretty girl and you're not going to change, so you might as well settle down and get used to it."

She sighed and then awkwardly slipped her coat off and let it hang on the chair behind her like a vegetable skin.

"I once tried wearing very baggy formless clothes, muu muus, but that didn't work because I got tired of looking like a slob. It's one thing to have this fleshy thing covering me but it's another thing to be called a beatnik at the same time."

Then she gave me a great big smile and said, "Anyway, that's my problem. Where do we go from here? What's next? Got any more candy bars?"

I pretended to get one from my pocket and she laughed out loud. It was a pleasing thing.

Suddenly she turned her attention upon me in a very strong way. "Why are you here in this funny library?" she said. "This place where losers bring their books. I'm curious about you now. What's your story, Mr. Candyman Librarian?"

She was smiling as she said these things.

"I work here," I said.

"That's too easy. Where did you come from? Where are you going?"

"Well, I've done all sorts of things," I said, sounding falsely old. "I worked in canneries, sawmills, factories, and now I'm here."

"Where do you live?"

"Here," I said.

"You live here in the library?" she said.

"Yes. I have a large room in the back with a small kitchen and toilet."

"Let me see it," she said. "I'm suddenly curious about you. A young-old man like yourself working in a creepy place like this doesn't show that you've come out too far ahead of the game either."

"You're really laying it on the line," I said, because she had really gotten to me.

"I'm that way," she said. "I may be sick, but I'm not stupid. Show me your room."

"Well," I said, dogging a little. "That's a little irregular."

"You're kidding," she said. "You mean there's something irregular for this place? I don't know how to break it to you, but you've got a pretty far-out operation going on here. This library is a little on the whacky side."

She stood up and stretched awkwardly, but it's hard to describe the rest of it. I had never in my life seen a woman graced with such a perfect body whose spell was now working on me. As certain as the tides in the sea rush to the shore, I showed her my room.

"I'd better get my coat," she said. She folded her coat over her arm. "After you, Mr. Librarian."

"I've never done this before," I said, faraway-like as if to no one.

"Neither have I," she said. "It will be a different thing for both of us."

I started to say something else, but abstraction clouded my tongue and made it distant and useless.

"The library isn't really open now, is it?" she said. "I mean, it's after midnight and it's only open for special books, latecomers like myself, right?"

"Yes, it's 'closed' but—"

"But what?" she said.

I don't know where that "but" came from but it vanished just as fast, returning to some conjunctional oblivion.

"But nothing," I said.

"You had better turn out the lights, then," she said. "You don't want to waste electricity."

"Yes," I said, feeling a door close behind me, knowing that somehow this at first-appearing shy unhappy girl was turning, turning into something strong that I did not know how to deal with.

"I'd better turn the lights out," I said.

"Yes," she said.

I turned the lights out in the library and turned the light on in my room. That was not all I was turning on as a door closed behind us and a door opened in front of us.

"Your room is very simple," she said, putting her coat down on my bed. "I like that. You must live a very lonely life with all the losers and dingalings, myself included, that bring their books in here."

"I call it home," I said.

"That's sad," she said. "How long have you been here?"

"Years," I said. What the hell.

"You're too young to have been here that long," she said. "How old are you?"

"Thirty-one."

"That's a good age."

She had her back to me and was staring at the cupboard in my kitchen.

"It's all right to look at me," she said, without turning her head the slightest. "For some strange reason I don't mind your looking at me. Actually, it makes me feel good, but stop acting like a bandit when you do it."

I laughed at that.

Suddenly she turned around and looked half at me, then directly at me and smiled gently. "I really have had a hard time of it."

"I think I can almost understand," I said.

"That's nice," she said. She reached up and brushed her long black hair, causing a storm of bat lightning to flash past her ears.

"I'd like some coffee," she said, looking at me.

"I'll put it on," I said.

"No, let me," she said. "I know how to make good coffee. It's my specialty. Just call me Queen Caffeine."

"Well, damn," I said, a little embarrassed. "I'm sorry but I only have instant."

"Then instant it is," she said. "That's the name of the game. Perhaps I have a way with instant coffee, too. You never can tell," smiling.

"I'll get the stuff for you," I said.

"Oh, no," she said. "Let me do it. I'm a little curious about this kitchen of yours. I want to find out more about you, and this little kitchen is a good place to start. I can see at a glance, though, that you are something like me. You're not at home in the world."

"At least let me get the coffee for you," I said. "It's—"

"Sit down," she said. "You make me nervous. Only one person can make instant coffee at a time. I'll find everything."

I sat down on the bed next to her coat.

She found everything and made the coffee as if she were preparing a grand meal. I have never seen such care and eloquence applied to a cup of instant coffee. It was almost as if making a cup of instant coffee were a ballet and she were a ballerina pirouetting between the spoon, the cups, the jar, and the pan full of boiling water.

She cleared the clutter from my table, but then

decided that we should have our coffee on the bed, because it was more comfortable.

We sat there on the bed, cozy as two bugs in a rug, drinking coffee and talking about our lives. She worked as a laboratory technician for a small institute that was studying the effects of various experiments on dogs in an attempt to solve some of the more puzzling questions of science.

"How did you get the job?" I said.

"Through an ad in the *Chronicle*."

"What happened at San Francisco State?"

"I got tired of it. One of my English teachers fell in love with me. I told him to buzz off, so he failed me. That made me mad, so I transferred to UC."

"And UC?"

"The same story. I don't know what it is about English teachers and me, but they fall like guillotines when they see me coming."

"Where were you born?"

"Santa Clara. All right, I've answered enough of your questions. Now tell me how you got this job. What's your story, Mr. Librarian?"

"I assumed possession of it."

"I take it then that there was no ad in the paper."

"Nope."

"How did you assume possession of it?"

"The fellow who was here before me couldn't stand children. He thought they were going to steal his shoes. I came in here with a book I had written and while he was writing it down in the Library Contents Ledger, a couple of children came in and he flipped, so I told him that I had better take over the library and he had better do something that didn't involve children. He told me he thought he was cracking up, too, and that's how I got this job."

"What did you do before you started working here?"

"I kicked around a lot: canneries, sawmills, factories. A woman supported me for a couple of years, then she got tired of it and kicked my ass out. I don't know," I said. "It was all pretty complicated before I started working here."

"What are you going to do after you quit here or do you plan on quitting?"

"I don't know," I said. "Something will come up. Maybe I'll get another job or find a woman to support me again or maybe I'll write a novel and sell it to the movies."

That amused her.

We had finished our coffee. It was funny because suddenly we both noticed that we did not have any more coffee to drink and we were sitting together on the bed.

"What are we going to do now?" she said. "We can't drink any more coffee and it's late."

"I don't know," I said.

"I guess it would be too corny for us to go to bed together," she said. "But I can't think of anything else that would be better to do. I don't want to go home and sleep by myself. I like you. I want to stay here with you tonight."

"It's a puzzler," I said.

"Do you want to sleep with me?" she said, not

looking at me, but not looking away either. Her eyes were somewhere in between half-looking at me and half-thinking about something else.

"We don't have any place else to go," I said. "I'd feel like a criminal if you left tonight. It's hard to sleep with strangers. I gave it up years ago, but I don't think we are really strangers. Do you?"

She turned her eyes 3/4 towards me.

"No, we're not strangers."

"Do you want to sleep with me?" I asked.

"I don't know what it is about you," she said. "But you make me feel nice."

"It's my clothes. They're relaxing. They've always been this way. I know how to get clothes that make people feel better when they're with me."

"I don't want to sleep with your clothes," she said, smiling.

"Do you want to sleep with me?" I said.

"I've never slept with a librarian before," she said, 99% toward me. The other 1% was waiting to turn. I saw it starting to turn.

"I brought a book in here tonight denouncing my own body as grotesque and elephant-like, but now I want to take this awkward machine and lie down beside you here in this strange library."

Counting toward Tijuana

WHAT an abstract thing it is to take your clothes off in front of a stranger for the very first time. It isn't really what we planned on doing. Your body almost looks away from itself and is a stranger to this world.

We live most of our lives privately under our clothes, except in a case like Vida whose body lived outside of herself like a lost continent, complete with dinosaurs of her own choosing.

"I'll turn the lights out," she said, sitting next to me on the bed.

I was startled to hear her panic. She seemed almost relaxed a few seconds before. My, how fast she could move the furniture about in her mind. I responded to this by firmly saying, "No, please don't."

Her eyes stopped moving for a few seconds. They came to a crashing halt like blue airplanes.

"Yes," she said. "That's a good idea. It will be very hard, but I have no other choice. I can't go on like this forever."

She gestured toward her body as if it were far away in some lonesome valley and she, on top of a mountain, looking down. Tears came suddenly to her eyes. There was now rain on the blue wings of the airplanes.

Then she stopped crying without a tear having left her eyes. I looked again and all the tears had vanished. "We have to leave the lights on," she said. "I won't cry. I promise."

I reached out and, for the first time in two billion years, I touched her. I touched her hand. My fingers went carefully over her fingers. Her hand was almost cold.

"You're cold," I said.

"No," she said. "It's only my hand."

She moved slightly, awkwardly toward me and rested her head on my shoulder. When her head touched me, I could feel my blood leap forward, my nerves and muscles stretch like phantoms toward the future.

My shoulder was drenched in smooth white skin and long bat-flashing hair. I let go of her hand and touched her face. It was tropical.

"See," she said, smiling faintly. "It was only my hand."

It was fantastic trying to work around her body, not wanting to startle her like a deer and have her go running off into the woods.

I poetically shifted my shoulder like the last lines of a Shakespearean sonnet (Love is a babe; then might I not say so, / To give full growth to that which still doth grow.) and at the same time lowered her back onto the bed.

She lay there looking up at me as I crouched forward, descending slowly, and kissed her upon the mouth as gently as I could. I did not want that first kiss to have attached to it the slightest gesture or flower of the meat market.

The Decision

IT'S a hard decision whether to start at the top or the bottom of a girl. With Vida I just didn't know where to begin. It was really a problem.

After she reached up awkwardly and put my face in a small container which was her hands and kissed me quietly again and again, I had to start somewhere.

She stared up at me all the time, her eyes never leaving me as if I were an airfield.

I changed the container and her face became a flower in my hands. I slowly let my hands drift down her face while I kissed her and then further down her neck to her shoulders.

I could see the future being moved in her mind while I arrived at the boundaries of her bosom. Her breasts were so large, so perfectly formed under her sweater that my stomach was standing on a step-ladder when I touched them for the first time.

Her eyes never left me and I could see in her eyes the act of my touching her breasts. It was like brief blue lightning.

I was almost hesitant in a librarian sort of way.

"I promise," she said, reaching up and awkwardly pressing my hands harder against her breasts. She of course had no idea what that did to me. The stepladder started swirling.

She kissed me again, but this time with her tongue. Her tongue slid past my tongue like a piece of hot glass.

A Continuing Decision

WELL, it had been my decision to start at the top and I was going to have to carry it out and soon we arrived at the time to take off her clothes.

I could tell that she didn't want to have anything to do with it. She wasn't going to help. It was all up to me.

Damn it.

It wasn't exactly what I had planned on doing when I started working at the library. I just wanted to take care of the books because the other librarian couldn't do it any more. He was afraid of children, but of course it was too late now to think about his fears. I had my own problems.

I had gone further than taking this strange awkward beautiful girl's book. I was now faced with taking her body which lay before me and had to have its clothes taken off, so we could join our bodies together like a bridge across the abyss.

"I need your help," I said.

She didn't say anything. She just continued staring at me. That brief blue lightning flashed again in her eyes, but it was relaxed at the edges.

"What can I do?" she said.

"Sit up, please," I said.

"All right."

She sat up awkwardly.

"Please put your arms up," I said.

"It's that simple, isn't it?" she said.

Whatever was happening I was certainly getting down to it. It would have been much simpler just to have kindly taken her book for the library and sent her on her way but that was history now or like the grammar of a forgotten language.

"How's this?" she said and then smiled. "I feel like a San Francisco bank teller."

"That's right," I said. "Just do what the note says," and I started her sweater gently off. It slid up her stomach and went on over her breasts, getting briefly caught on one of them, so I had to reach down and help it over the breast, and then her neck and face disappeared in the sweater and came out again when the sweater went off her fingers.

It was really fantastic the way she looked. I could have been hung up for a long time there, but I kept moving on, had to. It was my mission in life to take her bra off.

"I feel like a child," she said. She turned sideways from me, so I could get at the brassiere clasp in the back. I fumbled at the clasp for a few moments. I've never had much luck with brassieres.

"Want me to help?" she said.

"No, I can get it," I said. "It may take me a few days but I'll get it. Don't dishearten. There . . . *AH!*"

That made Vida laugh.

She did not need a bra at all. Her breasts stayed right up there after the bra left them like an extra roof on a house and joined her sweater. It was a difficult pile of clothes. Each garment was won in a strange war.

Her nipples were small and delicately colored in relationship to the large full expansion of her breasts. Her nipples were very gentle. They were another incongruity fastened like a door to Vida.

Then at the same time we both looked down at her boots, long and black and leather like a cloud of animals gathered about her feet.

"I'll take your boots off," I said.

I had finished with the top of her and now it was time to start on the bottom. There certainly are a lot of parts to girls.

I took off her boots and then I took off her socks. I liked the way my hands ran along her feet like water over a creek. Her toes were the cutest pebbles I have ever seen.

"Stand up, please," I said. We were really moving along now. She got awkwardly to her feet and I unzipped her skirt. I brought it down her hips to the floor and she stepped out of it and I put it on the pile of other battles.

I looked into her face before I took her panties off. Her features were composed and though there still flashed bolts of brief blue lightning in her eyes, her eyes remained gentle at the edges and the edges were growing.

I took her panties off and the deed was done. Vida was without clothes, naked, there.

"See?" she said. "This isn't me. I'm not here." She reached out and put her arms about my neck. "But I'll try to be here for you, Mr. Librarian."

Two (37-19-36) Soliloquies

"I JUST don't understand why women want bodies like this. The grotesqueness of them and they try so very hard to get these bodies, moving hell and high water with dieting, operations, injections, obscene undergarments to arrive at one of these damn things and then if they try everything and still can't get one, the dumb cunts fake it. Well, here's one they can have for free. Come and get it, you bitches.

"They don't know what they're getting into or maybe they like it. Maybe they're all pigs like the women who use these bodies to turn the tides of money: the movie stars, models, whores.

"Oh, Christ!

"I just can't see the fatal attraction that bodies

like this hold for men and women. My sister has my body: tall and skinny. All these layers are beyond me. These aren't my breasts. These aren't my hips. This isn't my ass. I'm inside of all this junk. Can you see me? Look hard. I'm in here, Mr. Librarian."

She reached out and put her arms about my neck and I put my hands upon her hips. We stood there looking at each other.

"I think you're wrong," I said. "Whether you like it or not, you're a very beautiful woman and you've got a grand container. It may not be what you want, but this body is in your keeping and you should take good care of it and with pride, too. I know it's hard but don't worry about what other people want and what they get. You've got something that's beautiful and try to live with it.

"Beauty is the hardest damn thing in the world to understand. Don't buy the rest of the world's juvenile sexual thirsts. You're a smart young lady and you'd better start using your head instead of your body because that's what you're doing.

"Don't be a fatalist winner. Life's a little too short to haul that one around. This body is you and you'd better get used to it because this is all she wrote for this world and you can't hide from yourself.

"This is you.

"Let your sister have her own body and start learning how to appreciate and use this one. I think you might enjoy it if you let yourself relax and get your mind out of other people's sewers.

"If you get hung up on everybody else's hang-ups, then the whole world's going to be nothing more than one huge gallows."

We kissed.

BOOK 3:

Calling the Caves

Calling the Caves

FORTUNATELY, I was able to get in touch with Foster up at the caves when Vida discovered that she was pregnant. Vida and I talked it over. The decision to have the abortion was arrived at without bitterness and was calmly guided by gentle necessity.

"I'm not ready to have a child yet," Vida said. "And neither are you, working in a kooky place like this. Maybe another time, perhaps for certain another time, but not now. I love children, but this isn't the time. If you can't give them the maximum of yourself, then it's best to wait. There are too many children in the world and not enough love. An abortion is the only answer."

"I think you're right," I said. "I don't know about this library being a kooky place, but we're not ready for a child yet. Perhaps in a few years. I think you should use the pill after we have the abortion."

"Yes," she said. "It's the pill from now on."

Then she smiled and said, "It looks like our bodies got us."

"It happens sometimes," I said.

"Do you know anything about this kind of business?" Vida said. "I know a little bit. My sister had an abortion last year in Sacramento, but before she had the abortion, she went to a doctor in Marin County who gave her some hormone shots, but they didn't work because it was too late. The shots work if you take them soon enough and they're quite a bit cheaper than an abortion."

"I think I'd better call Foster," I said. "He got into a thing like this last year and had to go down to Tijuana with one of his Indian girls."

"Who's Foster?" Vida said.

"He takes care of the caves," I said.

"What caves?"

"This building is too small," I said.

"What caves?" she said.

I guess I was rattled by the events in Vida's stomach. I hadn't realized it. I calmed myself down a little bit and said, "Yes, we have some caves up in Northern California where we store most of our books because this building is too small for our collection.

"This library is very old. Foster takes care of the caves. He comes down here every few months and loads his van up with books and stores them in the caves.

"He also brings me food and the little things that I need. The rest of the time he stays drunk and chases the local women, mostly Indians. He's quite a guy. A regular explosion of a man.

"He had to go down to Tijuana last year. He told me all about it. He knows a very good doctor there. There's a telephone at the caves. I'll give him a ring. I've never done it before. Never had to. Things are usually pretty calm down here. We might as well get this thing going. Would you watch the library while I do it?"

"Yes," Vida said. "Of course. It would be a privilege. I never thought that I would end up being the librarian of this place, but I guess I should have had an inkling when I came in here with my book under my arm."

She was smiling and wearing a short green dress. Her smile was on top of the dress. It looked like a flower.

"It will only take a few minutes," I said. "I think there's a pay telephone down at the corner. That is, if it's still there. I haven't been out of here in so long that they may have moved it."

"No, it's still there," Vida said, smiling. "I'll take care of everything. Don't worry. Your library is in good hands."

She held her hands out to me and I kissed them.

"See?" she said.

"You know how to put the books down in the Library Contents Ledger?" I said.

"Yes," she said. "I know how to do it and I'll give anyone who brings in a book the royal carpet treatment. Don't worry. Everything's going to be all right. Stop worrying, Mr. Librarian. I think you have been in here too long. I think I'll kidnap you soon."

"You could ask them to wait," I said. "I'll only be gone for a few minutes."

"Come on now!" Vida said. "Let your granny gland relax a little and slow down those rocking chair secretions."

Outside (Briefly)

GEE, it had been a long time. I hadn't realized that being in that library for so many years was almost like being in some kind of timeless thing. Maybe an eternity.

Actually being outside was quite different from looking out the window or the door. I walked down the street, feeling strangely awkward on the sidewalk. The concrete was too hard, aggressive or perhaps I was too light, passive.

It was something to think about.

I had a lot of trouble opening the telephone booth door but finally I got inside and started to call Foster up at the caves when suddenly I realized that I didn't have any money with me. I searched all my pockets but, alas, not a cent. I didn't need money in the library.

"Back already?" Vida said. She looked very pretty behind the counter in her green dress with her flower-like head.

"I don't have any money," I said.

After she stopped laughing, which took about five minutes, very funny, she went and got her purse and gave me a handful of change.

"You're too much," she said. "Are you sure you

haven't forgotten how to use money? You hold it like this." She held an imaginary coin between her fingers and started laughing all over again.

I left. I had my dime.

Foster's Coming

I CALLED Foster up at the caves. I could hear his telephone ringing. It rang seven or eight times and then Foster answered it.

"What's happening?" Foster said. "Who is this? What are you up to, you son-of-a-bitch? Don't you know it's one o'clock in the afternoon. What are you? A vampire?"

"It's me," I said. "You old drunk!"

"Oh," he said. "The kid. Hell, why didn't you say so? What's up down there? Somebody bring in an elephant with a book written on it? Well, feed it some hay and I'll be down with the van."

"Very funny, Foster," I said.

"Not bad," he said. "Nothing's impossible at that loony bin you've got down there. What's up, kid?"

"I've got a problem."

"You?" he said. "How in the hell can you have a problem? You're inside all the time. Is that prison pallor of yours beginning to flake?"

"No," I said. "My girlfriend is pregnant."

"DINGALING CUCKOO!" Foster said and the conversation stopped for a moment while Foster laughed so hard it almost shook the telephone booth hundreds of miles away.

Finally he stopped laughing and said, "It sounds like you've really been working hard at the library, but when did fornication become one of its services? Girlfriend, huh? Pregnant, huh? Cuckoo, kid!"

He started to laugh all over again. It was everybody's day to laugh except mine.

"Well, what do you need?" he said. "A little trip down to Tijuana? A short visit with my abortionist buddy, Dr. Garcia?"

"Something like that," I said.

"Well, I'll have a few drinks for breakfast," he said. "And get in the van and be in sometime late this evening."

"Good," I said. "That's what I need."

Then there was a slight pause at the cave end of the telephone.

"You don't have any money, do you, kid?" Foster said.

"Are you kidding?" I said. "Where would I get any money? This is the lowest-paying job in the world because it doesn't. I had to borrow this dime from my girlfriend to call you collect."

"I guess I'm still gorgonized," he said. "I don't know what I was thinking. I was probably thinking that I spent all my money last night on drink or was it last week? and I haven't got a cent. Cuckoo, have I been out of it!"

"What about my food?" I said, realizing that he had spent my food money, too.

"Is she good-looking?" Foster said. "Will she do in a dust storm at midnight with a candle?"

"What?" I said.

"I'll bring the money, then," he said. "It costs a couple of hundred if you make the good doctor toe the line. He likes to speculate sometimes—it's the businessman in him—but you can hold him down by putting the two hundred in his hand.

"Let's see: You'll need airplane tickets and walking around money and you might need a hotel room for her to rest up after she sees Dr. Garcia.

"I'll go down to the bar and turn a couple of the patrons upside down and see what I can shake out of their pockets, so you hang on, kid, and I'll be in late this evening and we'll get this show on the road.

"I never thought you had it in you, kid. Tell your young lady hello for me and that everything will be all right. Foster's coming."

Masturbation

THAT Foster! I went back to the library. Somebody was just leaving as I arrived. It was a young boy, maybe sixteen. He looked awfully tired and nervous. He hurried past me.

"Thank God, darling, you didn't get lost," Vida said. "I was worried that you wouldn't be able to find your way back up the block. It's great to see you, honey."

She came out from behind the desk and moved breathlessly to where I was given a great big lingering kiss. She had lost about 80% of her awkwardness since she had come to the library that evening late last year. The 20% she had left was very intriguing.

"How did it go?" she said.

"Fine," I said. "Here's your dime. Foster's on his way down. He'll be in late this evening."

"Good," she said. "I'll be glad when this thing is over. I wouldn't like to wait for an abortion. I'm glad we're doing it right now."

"So am I. Foster knows a great doctor," I said. "Everything will be all right. Foster's going to take care of everything."

"Fine, just fine," she said. "What about money? I have—"

"No, no," I said. "Foster will get the money."

"You're sure, because—"

"No, I'm sure," I said. "Who was that boy who was leaving?"

"Some kid who brought in a book," she said. "I welcomed it in my most pleasing manner and recorded it in my best handwriting in the Library Contents Ledger."

"Gee," I said. "This is the first time I haven't received a book in years."

"Oh, honey," she said. "You aren't that old, even

though you try to be, but that kind of thinking is going to make you an old man if you work at it hard enough."

She kissed me again.

"I'll take a look at it," I said.

"Your old age?" she said.

"No, the book."

She stood there and smiled after me as I walked over behind the desk and opened the Library Contents Ledger and read:

THE OTHER SIDE OF MY HAND by Harlow Blade, Jr. The author was about sixteen and seemed a little sadder than he should have been for his age. He was very shy around me. The poor dear. He kept looking at me out of the corner of his eye.

Finally he said, "Are *you* the librarian?"

"Yes," I said.

"I expected a man."

"He's out," I said. "So I'll just have to do. I don't bite."

"You're not a man," he said.

"What's your name?"

"What?"

"Your name, please? I have to write it down here in the ledger before we can take your book. You do have a name, don't you?"

"Yes. Harlow Blade, Jr."

"Now what's your book about? I have to have that, too. Just tell me what it's about and I'll write it down here in the ledger."

"I was expecting a man," he said.

"What's your book about? The subject, please?"

"Masturbation. I'd better be going now."

I started to thank him for bringing his book in and tell him that he could put it anywhere he wanted to in the library, but he left without saying anything else. Poor kid.

What a strange place this library is, but I guess it's the only place you can bring a book in the end. I brought mine here and I'm still here.

Vida trailed over to the desk and moved behind it with me and put her arm around me and read the entry over my shoulder after I finished reading it.

"I think it sounds pretty good," she said.

Gee, the handwriting of a different librarian lay before me on the desk. It was the first book I hadn't welcomed and recorded there myself in years.

I looked over at Vida for a moment. I must have looked at her kind of strangely because she said, "Oh, no. No, no, no."

Foster

FOSTER arrived at midnight. We were in my room, sitting around drinking coffee and talking about small casual things that are never remembered afterward, except perhaps in the twilight of our lives.

Foster never bothered to ring the bell on the front door. He said it made him think he was going into some kind of church and he'd had enough of that to last him forever.

BANG! BANG! BANG! he just slugged the door with his fist and I could always hear him and was afraid that he would break the glass. Foster couldn't be overlooked nor forgotten.

"What's that?" Vida said, jumping up startled from the bed.

"That's Foster," I said.

"It sounds like an elephant," she said.

"He never touches the stuff," I said.

We went out into the library and turned on the lights and there was Foster on the other side of the door, still banging away with that big fist of his.

There was a large smile on his face and he was wearing his traditional T-shirt. He never wore a shirt or a coat or a sweater. It didn't make any difference what the weather did. Cold, wind or rain, Foster always wore his T-shirt. He was of course sweating like a dam and his buffalo-heavy blond hair hung almost down to his shoulders.

"Hello!" he said. His voice came booming through as if the glass door were made of tissue paper. "What's going on in there?"

I opened the door for him and could see the van parked out in front. The van was big and strange and looked like a prehistoric animal asleep in front of the library.

"Well, here I am," he said and threw an arm around me and gave me a big hug. There was a bottle of whiskey in his other hand and half the whiskey was gone.

"How's it going, kid? Cheer up. Foster's here. Hey, *hello* there!" he said to Vida. "My, aren't you a pretty girl! Damn, am I glad I drove down here! Every mile was worth it. My God, ma'am, you're so pretty I'd walk ten miles barefooted on a freezing morning to stand in your shit."

Vida broke up. There was a big smile on her face. I could tell that she liked him instantly.

My, how her body had relaxed these few months we'd been going together. She was still a little awkward, but now instead of treating it as a handicap, she treated it as a form of poetry and it was fantastically charming.

Vida came over and put her arm around Foster. He gave her a great big hug, too, and offered her a drink from his bottle of whiskey.

"It's good for you," he said.

"All right, I'll give it a try," she said.

He wiped the mouth of the bottle off with his hand in the grand manner and offered her the bottle and she took a delicate nip.

"Hey, kid. You try some of this stuff, too. It'll grow hair on your books."

I took a drink.

Wow!

"Where did you get this whiskey?" I said.

"I bought it from a dead Indian."

The A D Standoff

"LEAD the way," Foster said.

He had his arm around Vida. They were like two peas in a pod. I was very pleased that they were getting along so well together. We went back to my room to relax and make our plans for Tijuana.

"Where have you been all my life?" Foster said.

"Not on the reservation," Vida said.

"Wonderful!" Foster said. "Where did you find this girl?"

"She came along," I said.

"I should be working down here at the library," Foster said. "Not up at the caves. I got up on the wrong side of the map. Hey, hey, you're the prettiest thing I've ever seen in my life. My God, you're even prettier than my mother's picture."

"It's the whiskey," Vida said. "I always look better through amber-colored fluid."

"Damn, it's the whiskey. You're pulling my 86 proof. I think I'll take over this library for a while and you kids can go up and dust off those God-damn books and live at the caves. It's real nice up there. But don't mention to anyone that you know me. Jesus Christ and old Foster wore out their welcome at the same time. I only survive on my good looks these days."

The Plan for Tijuana

WE went back to my room and we all sat down on the bed together and drank a little whiskey and made plans for Tijuana. I usually don't drink but I figured the present condition of our lives merited a little drink.

"Well, it's a little abortion, huh?" Foster said. "You're sure now?"

"Yeah," I said. "We talked it over. That's what we want."

Foster looked over at Vida.

"Yes," she said. "We're too immature right now to have a child. It would only confuse us and this confusion would not be good for a child. It's hard enough being born into this world without having immature and confused parents. Yes, I want the abortion."

"OK, then," Foster said. "There's nothing to be afraid of. I know a good doctor: Dr. Garcia. He won't hurt you and there will be no complications. Everything will be just fine."

"I trust you," she said.

Vida reached over and took my hand.

"The arrangements are very simple," Foster said. "You'll take a plane down there. There's one that leaves at 8:15 tomorrow morning for San Diego. I've got you both round-trip tickets. I called the doctor and he'll be waiting for you. You'll be in TJ before noon and the thing will be over in a short while.

"You can come back in the evening on the plane if you feel up to it, but it you want to stay over in San Diego, I've got a reservation for you at the Green Hotel. I know the guy who runs the place. He's a good guy. You'll feel a little weak after the abortion, so it's up to you if you want to stay. It just depends on how you feel, but don't push it if you feel too woozy, just stay over at the hotel.

"Sometimes Dr. Garcia tries to speculate on the price of the abortion, but I told him you were coming and you only had 200 dollars and there was no more and he said, 'OK, Foster, will do.' He doesn't speak very good English but he's very kind and very good. He's a regular doctor. He did me a good turn with that Indian girl last year. Any questions or anything? Damn! you're a pretty girl."

He gave Vida a nice hug.

"I think you've probably covered it all," I said.

"Vida?" he said.

"No, I can't think of anything."

"What about the library?" I said.

"Whatabout the library?" Foster said.

"Who's going to watch it? There has to be somebody here. That's a big part of this library. Somebody has to be here twenty-four hours a day to receive and welcome books. It's the very foundation of this library. We can't close it. It has to remain open."

"You mean me?" Foster said. "Oh, no. I'm strictly a caveman. You'll have to get another boy."

"But there has to be somebody here," I said, looking hard at him.

"Oh, no," Foster said.

"But," I said.

Vida was awfully amused by the whole thing. I was fully aware that Vida did not share the intensity of my feeling toward the library. I could understand that it was a rather strange calling that I had answered, but it was a thing I had to do.

"I'm a caveman," Foster said.

"This is our job," I said. "This is what we were hired to do. We have to take care of this library and the people that need its services."

"I was meaning to bring that up," Foster said.

"This is a kind of slow-paying operation. I haven't been paid in two years. I'm supposed to make $295.50 a month."

"Foster!" I said.

"I was just joking," Foster said. "Just a little joke. Here, have some more whiskey."

"Thanks."

"Vida?" Foster said.

"Yes," she said. "Another sip would be just wonderful. It's relaxing."

"It's the old Indian tranquilizer," Foster said.

"You can take care of this place for a day or so while we're down in Mexico getting the abortion," I said. "It won't kill you to actually put in a day's work. It's been years since you've turned a wheel."

"I have my work up at the caves," he said. "It's quite a responsibility lugging books up there and putting them away, guarding them and making sure cave seepage doesn't get to them."

"Cave seepage!" I said, horrified.

"Forget I said that," Foster said. "I don't want to go into it right now, but OK, I'll stay here and take care of the library until you get back. I don't like it but I'll do it."

"Cave seepage?" I repeated.

"What do I have to do around here?" Foster said. "How do I deal with the nuts that bring their books in? What do you do here, anyway? Have some whiskey. Tell me all about it."

Vida was very amused by what was going on. She certainly was pretty. We were all very relaxed lying there on the bed. The whiskey had made us mud-puddly at the edges of our bodies and the edges of our minds.

"This is delightful," Vida said.

Foster's Girl #1

"WHAT's that?" Foster said, almost moving on the bed.

"That's the bell," I said. "Somebody is out there with a new book for the library. I'll show you how we honor a book into the library. 'Welcome it' is the phrase I use."

"Sounds like a funeral parlor," Foster said. "Damn, what time is it?" Foster looked around the room. "I can hear it ticking."

I looked over at the clock. Foster couldn't see it because of the way he was lying on the bed.

"After midnight."

"That's kind of late to bring a book in, isn't it? Midnight? That's twelve."

"We're open twenty-four hours a day, seven days a week. We never close," I said.

"Good God!" Foster said.

"See what I mean?" Vida said.

"Do I," Foster said. "This boy needs a rest."

Then he looked over at Vida. He appraised her

in a classic computerized masculine manner without being obvious or sensual and he liked what he saw.

Vida looked at him smiling gently without disturbing her mouth. It remained unchanged by her smile. I believe this thing has been gone into before.

She was not the same girl who had brought her book in a few months before. She had become somebody else with her body.

"Yes," Foster said, finally. "Yes, maybe we had better go out and see who's bringing in a book. We don't want to keep her, I mean, them waiting. It's cold outside."

Foster had never been aware of cold in his entire life, so he was a little drunk and his imagination had just gone into full gallop.

"What do you do out there?" Foster said. "Maybe I'll just go out there and take care of it myself. You kids can sit here and relax. No reason to stop being comfortable when old Foster's around. I'll take care of that book myself. Besides, I have to find out what's going on here if I'm going to run this asylum while you're in TJ."

Vida's smile had opened until now you could see the immaculate boundaries of her teeth. Her eyes had small friendly lightning walking across them.

I was smiling, too.

"What do you do out there? You write down the title of the book and the name of the writer and a little something about the book into that big black ledger, huh?"

"That's right," I said. "And you have to be friendly, too. That's important. To make the person and the book feel wanted because that's the main purpose of the library and to gather pleasantly together the unwanted, the lyrical and haunted volumes of American writing."

"You're kidding," Foster said. "You have to be kidding."

"Come on, Foster," I said. "Or I'll bring up 'cave seepage' again. You know 'cave seepage.' "

"All right. All right. All right, cuckoo," Foster said. "I'll be on my best and besides, who knows: I might want to be on my best. I'm not such a bad guy. Come to think of it, I've got a lot of friends. They may not admit it, but I'm a big place in their hearts."

The bell was still ringing but it was growing weak and needed immediate attention. Foster was by now off the bed. He ran his hand through his buffalo-heavy blond hair as if to comb it before going out to the library.

Blank like Snow

WHILE Foster went into the library to welcome his first book, Vida and I continued lying there on the bed taking little nips from the bottle of whiskey he had graciously left behind. After a while Vida and I were so relaxed that we both could have been rented out as fields of daisies.

Suddenly, we had lost track of time, Foster came slamming into the room. He was very angry in his overweight T-shirt sweating kind of way.

"I think we'd better close this nuthouse while you're south," he said, demanding whiskey with his right hand. "Come to think of it, we should close this God-damn place forever. Everybody go home. Pick up their marbles. That is, if they have any left."

Foster gobbled down a big turkey slug of whiskey. He grimaced and shook when it hit his stomach. "That's better," he said, wiping his hand across his mouth.

"What happened?" Vida said. "It looks like your library vaccination didn't take."

"You're telling me. More whiskey!" Foster said, addressing the bottle as if it were a healing hand of balm.

"I hope you didn't frighten them," I said. "That's not the purpose of this library. It's a service, not a demand that we perform here."

"Frighten them? Are you kidding, kid? It was the other God-damn way around. Hell, I usually get along with people."

"What happened?" Vida repeated.

"Well, I went out there and it wasn't exactly who I expected would be there. I mean, they were standing outside and—"

"Who was it?" Vida said.

"A woman?" I said, a little mercilessly.

"It's not important," Foster said. "Let me continue, damn it! Yes, there was a woman out there and I use the word woman with serious reservation. She was ringing the bell and she had a book under her arm, so I opened the door. That was a mistake."

"What did she look like?" I said.

"It's not important," Foster said.

"Come on," Vida said. "Tell us."

Ignoring us, Foster continued telling the story in his own manner, "When I opened the door she opened her mouth at the same time. 'Who are you?' she demanded to know in a voice just like a car wreck. What the hell!

" 'I'm Foster,' I said.

" 'You don't look like any Foster I've ever seen,' she said. 'I think you're somebody else because you're no Foster.'

" 'That's my name,' I said. 'I've always been Foster.'

" 'Haa! but enough of you. Where's my mother?' she demanded.

" 'What do you mean, your mother? You're too old to have a mother,' I said. I was tired of humoring the bag.

" 'What do you want done with that book?' I said.

" 'That's none of your God-damn business, you impostor Foster. Where's she at?"

" 'Good night,' I said.

" 'What do you mean, good night? I'm not going anywhere. I'm staying right here until you tell me about my mother.'

" 'I don't know where your mother is and frankly, to quote Clark Gable in *Gone with the Wind,* "I don't give a damn." '

" 'Call my mother Clark Gable!' she said, and then she tried to slap me. Well, that was quite enough out of her, so I grabbed her hand in mid-flight and spun her around and gave her a big shove out the door. She went flying out that door like a garbage can on the wing.

" 'Let my mother go free!' she yelled. 'My mother! My mother!'

"I started to close the door. It was getting kind of dreamlike about this time. I didn't know whether to wake up or slug the bitch.

"She made a threatening motion toward the glass, so I went outside and escorted her down the stairs. We had a little struggle along the way, but I laid a little muscle on her arm and she cooled it and at the same time I gentlemanly offered to break her chicken neck if she didn't take out down the street as fast as her clotheshanger legs would take her.

"The last I saw of her she was yelling, 'It isn't right that I should end up like this, doing these crazy things that I do, feeling the way I do, saying these things,' and she was tearing pages out of the book and throwing them over her head like a bride at a wedding reception."

"Like a bride at a wedding?" Vida said.

"The flowers," Foster said.

"Oh, I didn't understand," she said.

"I don't understand either," Foster said. "I went down and picked up some of the pages to see what kind of book they came from, but the pages didn't have any writing on them. They were blank like snow."

"That's how it goes here sometimes," I said. "We get some disturbed authors, but most of the time it's quiet. All you have to do is be patient with them and write down the author of the book, its title and a little description in the Library Contents Ledger, and let them put the book any place they want in the library."

"That's easy enough with this one," Foster said.

I started to say something—

"The description," Foster said.

I started to say something—

"Blank like snow," Foster said.

The Van

"I'LL sleep in my van," Foster said.

"No, there's room in here for you," I said.

"Please stay," Vida said.

"No, no," Foster said. "I'm more comfortable in my van. I always sleep there. I got a little mattress and a sleeping bag and it makes me cozy as a bug in a rug.

"No, it's already settled. It's the van for old Foster. You kids get a good night's sleep because you have to leave early on the plane. I'll take you down to the airfield."

"No, you can't do that," I said. "We'll have to

take the bus because you have to stay here and watch the library. Remember? It has to remain open all the time we're gone. You'll have to stay until we get back."

"I don't know about that," Foster said. "After that experience I had a little while ago, I don't know. You couldn't get somebody to come in from one of those temporary employment agencies to handle it, a Kelly Girl or something like that, huh? Hell, I'd pay for it out of my own pocket. They can take care of the library while I go down to North Beach and take in a few topless shows while I'm here."

"No, Foster," I said. "We can't trust this library to just anyone. You'll have to stay here while we're gone. We're not going to be gone long."

"Humor him, Foster," Vida said.

"OK. I wonder what the next nut will be about who brings a book in."

"Don't worry," I said. "That was an exception. Things will run smoothly while we're gone."

"I'll bet."

Foster got ready to go outside. "Here, have another drink of whiskey," Foster said. "I'm going to take the bottle with me."

"When does the plane leave?" Vida said.

"8:15," Foster said. "Our pal here can't drive, so I guess you'll have to take the bus because the Library Kid here wants me to stay and tend his garden of nuts."

"I can drive," Vida said, looking smoothly-beautiful and young.

"Can you drive a van?" Foster said.

"I think so," she said. "I used to drive trucks and pickups one summer when I was on a ranch in Montana. I've always been able to drive anything that's got four wheels, sports cars, anything. I even drove a school bus once, taking some kids on a picnic."

"A van's different," Foster said.

"I've driven a horse van," Vida said.

"This isn't a horse van," Foster said, now somewhat outraged. "There's never been a horse in my van!"

"Foster," Vida said. "Don't get mad, dear. I was just telling you that I can drive it. I can drive anything. I've never been in an accident. I'm a good driver. That's all. You have a beautiful van."

"It is a good one," Foster said, now placated. "Well, I guess I don't see any harm in it and it would get you out there a lot faster than the bus and you could get back here faster. It would be a lot smoother ride. Buses are horrible, and you can park it right out there at the airfield. I guess I won't need the van while I'm working at this God-damn madhouse. Sure, you can take it, but drive carefully. There's only one van like that in the whole world and she's mine and I love her."

"Don't worry," Vida said. "I'll love it, too."

"Good deal," Foster said. "Well, I guess I'd better go out and get to bed. Any more whiskey here?"

"No, I think we've had enough," I said.

"OK."

"Do you want us to wake you?" Vida said.

"No, I'll be up," Foster said. "I can get up when I want to, down to the minute. I've got an alarm clock in my head. It always gets me up. Oh, I almost forgot to tell you something. Don't eat anything for breakfast tomorrow. It's against the rules."

Johnny Cash

AFTER Foster left to go out and spend the night in his van, we started getting ready for tomorrow. We wouldn't have much time in the morning when we woke up.

Vida had enough clothes there at the library, so she wouldn't have to go home. Even though she only lived a block from the library, I of course had never been there. Sometimes in the past I had been curious about her place and she told me about it.

"It's very simple," she told me. "I don't have much. All I have is a few books on a shelf, a white rug, a little marble table on the floor, and some records for my stereo: Beatles, Bach, Rolling Stones, Byrds, Vivaldi, Wanda Landowska, Johnny Cash. I'm not a beatnik. It's just that I always considered my body to be more possessions than I ever needed and so everything else had to be simple."

She packed a few clothes for us in an old KLM

bag and our toothbrushes and my razor in case we had to stay overnight in San Diego.

"I've never had an abortion before," Vida said. "I hope we don't have to stay overnight in San Diego. I was there once and I didn't like it. There are too many unlaid sailors there and everything is either stone stark or neon cheap. It's not a good town."

"Don't worry about it," I said. "We'll just play it by ear and if everything's all right, we'll come back tomorrow evening."

"That sounds reasonable," Vida said, finishing with our simple packing.

"Well, let's have a kiss, honey, and go to bed. We need some sleep," I said. "We're both tired and we have to get up early in the morning."

"I'll have to take a bath and a douche," Vida said. "And put a little dab of perfume behind my ears."

I took Vida in my arms and gathered the leaves and blossoms of her close, a thing she returned to me, delicate and bouquet-like.

Then we took off our clothes and got into bed. I put out the light and she said, "Did you set the clock, honey?"

"Oh, I forgot," I said. "I'll get up."

"I'm sorry," she said.

"No," I said. "I should have remembered to set the clock. What time do you want to wake up? Six?"

"No, I think you'd better make it 5:30. I want to take care of my 'female complaints' before Foster wakes up, so I can cook a good breakfast for all of us. It'll be a long day and we'll need a solid start."

"The lady is not for breakfast," I said. "Remember what Foster said?"

"Oh. Oh, that's right. I forgot," Vida said.

It was hard for a minute and then we both smiled across the darkness at what we were doing. Though we could not see our smiles, we knew they were there and it comforted us as dark-night smiles have been doing for thousands of years for the problemed people of the earth.

I got up and turned the light on. Vida was still smiling softly as I set the clock for 5:30. It was absolutely too late for remorse now or to cry against the Fates. We were firmly in the surgical hands of Mexico.

"Genius"

VIDA did not look at all pregnant as she got into her bath. Her stomach was still so unbelievably thin that it was genius and I wondered how there could be enough intestines in there to digest any food larger than cookies or berries.

Her breasts were powerful but delicate and wet at the nipples.

She had put a pot of coffee on before she had gotten into the tub and I was standing there watching it perk and watching her bathe at the same time through the open door of the bathroom.

She had her hair piled and pinned on top of her head. It looked beautiful resting on the calm of her neck.

We were both tired, but not as nervous as we could have been facing the prospects of the day, because we had gone into a gentle form of shock that makes it easier to do one little thing after another, fragile step by fragile step, until you've done the big difficult thing waiting at the end, no matter what it is.

I think we have the power to transform our lives into brand-new instantaneous rituals that we calmly act out when something hard comes up that we must do.

We become like theaters.

I was taking turns watching the coffee perk and watching Vida at her bath. It was going to be a long day but fortunately we would get there only moment by moment.

"Is the coffee done yet?" Vida said.

I smelled the coffee fumes that were rising like weather from the spout. They were dark and heavy with coffee. Vida had taught me how to smell coffee. That was the way she made it.

I had always been an instant man, but she had taught me how to make real coffee and it was a good thing to learn. Where had I been all those years, thinking in terms of coffee as dust?

I thought about making coffee for a little while as

I watched it perk. It's strange how the simple things in life go on while we become difficult.

"Honey, did you hear me?" Vida said. "The coffee. Stop daydreaming and get on the coffee, dear. Is it done?"

"I was thinking about something else," I said.

Foster's Bell

VIDA put on a simple but quite attractive white blouse with a short blue skirt—you could see easily above her knees—and a little half-sweater thing on over the blouse. I've never been able to describe clothes so that anyone knows what I am talking about.

She did not have any make-up on except for her eyes. They looked dark and blue in the way that we like eyes to look in these last years of the seventh decade of the Twentieth Century.

I heard the silver bell ringing on the library door. The bell was ringing rapidly in a kind of shocked manner. The bell seemed almost frightened and crying for help.

It was Foster.

Foster had never really taken to that bell. He had always insisted that it was a sissy bell and always offered to put a bell up himself. He continued the thing as I let him in. I opened the door but he stood there with his hand on the bell rope, though he was not ringing the bell any more.

It was still dark and Foster was wearing his eternal T-shirt and his buffalo-heavy blond hair hung about his shoulders.

"You should take my advice," he said. "Get rid of this damn bell and let me put a real bell up for you."

"We don't want a bell that will frighten people," I said.

"What do you mean frighten people? How in the hell can a bell frighten people?"

"We need a bell that fits the service we offer, that blends in with the library. We need a gentle bell here."

"No roughneck bells, huh?" Foster said.

"I wouldn't put it that way," I said.

"Hell," Foster said. "This bell rings like a God-damn queer down on Market Street. What are you running here?"

"Don't worry about it," I said.

"Well, I'm just trying to look out for your best interests. That's all, kid." He reached over and gave the bell a little tap on its butt.

"Foster!" I said.

"Hell, kid, a tin can and a spoon make a great bell."

"What about a fork and a knife and a bowl of soup to go with it, Foster? A little mashed potatoes and gravy and maybe a turkey leg? What about that? Wouldn't that make a good bell?"

"Forget it," Foster said. He reached over and gave the bell another little tap on its silver butt and said, "Good-bye, sweetie."

The TJ Briefing

VIDA cooked Foster and me a good breakfast, though she didn't have anything with us except some coffee.

"You certainly look pretty this morning," Foster said. "You look like a dream I've never had before."

"I bet you tell that to all the girls," Vida said. "I can see that you're a flirt from way back."

"I've had a girlfriend or two," Foster said.

"Some more coffee?" Vida said.

"Yeah, another cup of coffee would be fine. Sure is good coffee. Somebody here knows their way around coffee beans."

"What about you, honey?" Vida said.

"Sure."

"There you go."

"Thank you."

Vida sat back down.

"Well, you know what you're supposed to do,"

Foster said after breakfast. "There's nothing to worry about. Dr. Garcia is a wonderful doctor. There will be no pain or fuss. Everything will go just beautifully. You know how to get there. It's just a few blocks off the Main Street of town.

"The doc may want to try and get a few extra bucks out of you, but hold the line and say, "Well, Doctor Garcia, Foster said that it was 200 dollars and that's all we brought and here it is,' and take it out of your pocket.

"He'll look a little nervous and then he'll take it and put it in his pocket without counting it and then he's just like the best doctor in the whole wide world. Have faith in him and do what he says and relax and everything will be all right.

"He's a wonderful doctor. He saves a lot of people a lot of trouble."

The Library Briefing

". . . ," I said.

"I promise I won't take down that swishy little bell of yours with the silver pants and put up a tin can with a spoon, which would be the best bell for this asylum. Have you ever heard one?" Foster said.

". . . ," I said.

"I'm sorry about that. It's an awfully pretty sound.

So beautiful to the spirit and so soothing to the nerves."

"...," I said.

"That's a real shame," Foster said.

"...," I said.

"I didn't know you felt that way about it," Foster said.

"...," I said.

"Don't worry, I won't harm a brick on this library's head. I'll treat your library like a child's birthday cake in a little yellow box that I'm carrying home in my arms from the bakery because carrying it by the string would be too risky.

"I've got to be careful of that dog up ahead. He might bite me and I'd drop the cake. There, I'm past him. Good dog.

"Oh, oh, there's a little lady coming toward me. Got to be careful. She might have a heart attack and collapse in front of me and I might trip over her body. I won't take my eyes off her. There, she's passing me. Everything's going to be all right. Your library is safe," Foster said.

"...," Vida said, laughing.

"Thank you, honey," Foster said.

"...," I said.

"I love this place," Foster said.

"...," I said.

"I'll treat your patrons like saintly eggshells. I won't break one of them," Foster said.

"...," Vida said, laughing.

"Oh, honey, you're too nice," Foster said.

"...," I said.

"Stop worrying, kid. I know what I'm supposed to do and I'll do it the best I can and that's all I can say," Foster said.

". . . ," Vida said.

"Isn't it the truth and he's not old either. He's just a kid," Foster said.

". . . ," I said.

"I don't think I ever really appreciated the peace and quiet, the downhomeness of the caves until now. You've opened up a whole new world for me, kid. I should get down on my hands and knees and thank you with all my heart for what you've done."

". . . ," I said.

"Ah, California!" Foster said.

Foster's Heart

FOSTER insisted on carrying our bag out to the van. It was light and halfway through the dawn. Foster was busy sweating away in his T-shirt, even though we found the morning to be a little chilly.

During the years that I had known Foster, I'd never seen him when he wasn't sweating. It was probably brought about by the size of his heart. I was always certain that his heart was as big as a cantaloupe and sometimes I went to sleep thinking about the size of Foster's heart.

Once Foster's heart appeared to me in a dream. It was on the back of a horse and the horse was going into a bank and the bank was being pushed off a cloud. I couldn't see what was pushing the bank off, but it's strange to think *what* would push a bank off a cloud with Foster's heart in it, falling past the sky.

"What do you have in this bag?" Foster said. "It's so light I don't think there's anything in it."

He was following after Vida who led the way with a delightful awkwardness, looking so perfect and beautiful as not to be with us, as to be alone in some different contemplation of the spirit or an animal stepladder to religion.

"Never you mind our secrets," Vida said, not turning back.

"How would you like to visit my rabbit trap someday?" Foster said.

"And be your Bunny girl?" Vida said.

"I guess you've heard that one," Foster said.

"I've heard them all."

"I'll bet you have," Foster said, falling cleanly past the sky.

Vida Meets the Van

THERE were leftover pieces of blank white paper on the sidewalk from the woman last night. They looked terribly alone. Foster put our little bag in the van.

"There's your bag in the van. Now you're sure you know how to drive this thing?" Foster said. "It's a van."

"Yes, I know how to drive a van. I know how to drive anything that has wheels. I've even flown an airplane," Vida said.

"An airplane?" Foster said.

"I flew one up in Montana a few summers ago. It was fun," Vida said.

"You don't look like the airplane-flying type," Foster said. "Hell, a few summers ago you were in the cradle. Are you sure you weren't flying a stuffed toy?"

"Don't worry about your van," Vida said, returning the conversation from the sky to the ground.

"You've got to drive carefully," Foster said. "This van has its own personality."

"It's in good hands," Vida said. "My God, you're almost as bad with your van as he is with his library."

"Damn! all right," Foster said. "Well, I've told

you what to do and now I guess you'd better go and do it. I'll stay here and take care of the asylum while you're gone. I imagine it won't be dull if that lady I met last night is any example of what's going on here."

There were pieces of white paper on the ground.

Foster put his arms around both of us and gave us a very friendly, consoling hug as if to say with his arms that everything was going to be all right and he would see us in the evening.

"Well, kids, good luck."

"Thank you very much," Vida said, turning and giving Foster a kiss on the cheek. They looked heroically like father and daughter around each other's arms and cheek to cheek in the classic style that has brought us to these years.

"In you go," Foster said.

We got into the van. It suddenly felt awfully strange for me to be in a vehicle again. The metallic egg-like quality of the van was very surprising and in some ways I had to discover the Twentieth Century all over again.

Foster stood there on the curb carefully watching Vida at the controls of the van.

"Ready?" she said, turning toward me with a little smile on her face.

"Yeah, it's been a long time," I said. "I feel as if I'm in a time machine."

"I know," she said. "Just relax. I know what I'm doing."

"All right," I said. "Let's go."

Vida started the van as if she had been born to

the instrument panel, to the wheel and to the pedals.

"Sounds good," Vida said.

Foster was pleased with her performance, nodding at her as if she were an equal. Then he gave her the go signal and she took it and we were off to visit Dr. Garcia who was waiting for us that very day in Tijuana, Mexico.

BOOK 4:

Tijuana

The Freewayers

I HAD forgotten how the streets in San Francisco go to get to the freeway. Actually, I had forgotten how San Francisco went.

It was really a surprise to be outside again, travelling in a vehicle again. It had been almost three years. My God, I was twenty-eight when I went into the library and now I was thirty-one years old.

"What street is this?" I said.

"Divisadero," Vida said.

"Oh, yeah," I said. "It's Divisadero all right."

Vida looked over at me very sympathetically. We were stopped at a red light, next to a place that sold flying chickens and spaghetti. I had forgotten that there were places like that.

Vida took one hand off the wheel and gave me a little pat on the knee. "My poor dear hermit," she said.

We drove down Divisadero and saw a man washing the windows of a funeral parlor with a garden hose. He was spraying the hose against the second-floor windows. It was not a normal thing to see, so early in the morning.

Then Vida made a turn off Divisadero and went around the block. "Oak Street," she said. "You remember Oak Street? It'll take us to the freeway and down to the airport. You remember the airport, don't you?"

"Yes," I said. "But I've never been on an airplane. I've gone out there with friends who were going on airplanes, but that was years ago. Have the airplanes changed any?"

"Oh, honey," she said. "When we're through with all this, I've got to get you out of that library. I think you've been there long enough. They'll have to get somebody else."

"I don't know," I said, trying to drop the subject. I saw a Negro woman pushing an empty Safeway grocery cart on Oak Street. The traffic was very good all around us. It frightened me and excited me at the same time. We were headed for the freeway.

"By the way," Vida said. "Who do you work for?"

"What do you mean?" I said.

"I mean, who pays the bills for your library?" she said. "The money that it takes to run the place? The tab."

"We don't know," I said, pretending that was the answer to the question.

"What do you mean, you don't know?" Vida said. It hadn't worked.

"They send Foster a check from time to time. He never knows when it's coming or how much it will be. Sometimes they don't send us enough."

"They?" she said, keeping right on it.

We stopped for a red light. I tried to find something to look at. I didn't like talking about the financial structure of the library. I didn't like to think in terms of the library and money together. All I saw was a Negro man delivering papers from still another cart.

"Who are you talking about?" Vida said. "Who picks up the tab?"

"It's a foundation. We don't know who's behind it."

"What's the name of the foundation?" Vida said.

I guess that wasn't enough.

"The American Forever, Etc."

"The American Forever, Etc.," Vida said. "Wow! That sounds like a tax dodge. I think your library is a tax write-off."

Vida was now smiling.

"I don't know," I said. "All I know is that I have to be there. It's my job. I have to be there."

"Honey, I think you've got to get some new work. There must be something else that you can do."

"There are a lot of things I can do," I said, a little defensively.

Just then we slammed onto the freeway and my stomach flew into birds with snakes curling at their wings and we joined the mainstream of American motor thought.

It was frightening after so many years. I felt like a dinosaur plucked from my grave and thrust into competition with the freeway and its metallic fruit.

"If you don't want to work, honey," Vida said, "I think I can take care of us until you feel like it, but you've got to get out of that library as soon as possible. It's not the right place for you any more."

I looked out the window and saw a sign with a chicken holding a gigantic egg.

"I've got other things on my mind right now," I said, trying to get away. "Let's talk about it in a few days."

"You're not worried about the abortion, are you, honey?" Vida said. "Please don't be. I have perfect faith in Foster and his doctor. Besides, my sister had an abortion last year in Sacramento and she went to work the next day. She felt a little tired but that was all, so don't worry. An abortion is a rather simple thing."

I turned and looked at Vida. She was staring straight ahead after saying that, watching the traffic in front of us as we roared out of San Francisco down the freeway past Potrero Hill and toward the airplane that waited to fly us at 8:15 down California to land in San Diego at 9:45.

"Maybe when we get back we can go live at the caves for a while," Vida said. "It'll be spring soon. They should be pretty."

"Seepage," I said.

"What?" Vida said. "I didn't hear you. I was watching that Chevrolet up there to see what it was going to do. What did you say now, honey?"

"Nothing," I said.

"Anyway," she said. "We've got to get you out of that library. Maybe the best thing would be just to give the whole thing up, forget the caves and start someplace new together. Maybe we can go to New York or we'll move to Mill Valley or get an apartment on Bernal Heights or I'll go back to UC and get my degree and we'll get a little place in Berkeley. It's nice over there. You'd be a hero."

Vida seemed to be more interested in getting me out of the library than worrying about the abortion.

"The library is my life," I said. "I don't know what I'd do without it."

"We're going to fix you up with a new life," Vida said.

I looked down the freeway to where the San Francisco International Airport waited, looking almost medieval in the early morning like a castle of speed on the entrails of space.

The San Francisco International Airport

VIDA parked the van near the Benny Bufano statue of Peace that waited for us towering above the cars like a giant bullet. The statue looked at rest in that sea of metal. It is a steel thing with gentle mosaic and marble people on it. They were trying to tell us something. Unfortunately, we didn't have time to listen.

"Well, here we are," Vida said.

"Yeah."

I got our bag and we left the van there quite early

in the morning, planning, if everything went well, to pick it up that evening. The van looked kind of lonesome like a buffalo next to the other cars.

We walked over to the terminal. It was filled with hundreds of people coming and going on airplanes. The air was hung with nets of travelling excitement and people were entangled within them and we became a part of the catch.

The San Francisco International Airport Terminal is gigantic, escalator-like, marble-like, cybernetic-like and wants to perform a thing for us that we don't know if we're quite ready for yet. It is also very *Playboy*.

We went over—over being very large—and got our tickets from the Pacific Southwest Airlines booth. There was a young man and woman there. They were beautiful and efficient. The girl looked as if she would look good without any clothes on. She did not like Vida. They both had pins with half-wings on their chests like amputated hawks. I put our tickets in my pocket.

Then I had to go to the toilet.

"Wait here for me, honey," I said.

The toilet was so elegant that I felt as if I should have been wearing a tuxedo to take a leak.

Three men made passes at Vida while I was gone. One of them wanted to marry her.

We had forty-five minutes or so before our airplane left for San Diego, so we went and got a cup of coffee. It was so strange to be among people again. I had forgotten how complex they were in large units.

Everybody was of course looking at Vida. I had never seen a girl attract so much attention before. It was just as she said it would be: plus so.

A young handsome man in a yellow coat like a God-damn maître d' showed us to a table that was next to a plant with large green leaves. He was extremely interested in Vida, though he tried not to be obvious about it.

The basic theme of the restaurant was red and yellow with a surprising number of young people and the loud clatter of dishes. I had forgotten that dishes could be that noisy.

I looked at the menu, even though I wasn't hungry. It had been years since I had looked at a menu. The menu said good morning to me and I said good morning back to the menu. We could actually end our lives talking to menus.

Every man in the restaurant had been instantly alerted to Vida's beauty and the women, too, in a jealous sort of way. There was a green aura about the women.

A waitress wearing a yellow dress with a cute white apron took our order for a couple cups of coffee and then went off to get them. She was pretty but Vida made her pale.

We looked out the window to see airplanes coming and going, joining San Francisco to the world and then taking it away again at 600 miles an hour.

There were Negro men in white uniforms doing the cooking while wearing tall white hats, but there were no Negroes in the restaurant eating. I guess Negroes don't take airplanes early in the morning.

The waitress came back with our coffee. She put the coffee on the table and left. She had lovely blond hair but it was to no avail. She took the menu with her: good-bye, good morning.

Vida knew what I was thinking because she said, "You're seeing it for the first time. It really used to bother me until I met you. Well, you know all about that."

"Have you ever thought about going into the movies or working here at the airport?" I said.

That made Vida laugh which caused a boy about twenty-one years old to spill his coffee all over himself and the pretty waitress to rush a towel over to him. He was cooking in his own coffee.

It was time now to catch our airplane, so we left the restaurant. I paid a very pretty cashier at the front of the cafe. She smiled at me as she took the money. Then she looked at Vida and she stopped smiling.

There was much beauty among the women working in the terminal, but Vida was chopping it down almost as if it weren't even there. Her beauty, like a creature unto itself, was quite ruthless in its own way.

We walked to catch our plane causing people in pairs to jab each other with their elbows to bring the other's attention to Vida. Vida's beauty had probably caused a million black and blue marks: Ah, de Sade, thy honeycomb of such delights.

Two four-year-old boys walking with their mother suddenly became paralyzed from the neck up as they passed us. They did not take their eyes off Vida. They couldn't.

We walked down to the PSA pre-flight lounge stimulating pandemonium among the males our path chanced to cross. I had my arm around Vida, but it wasn't necessary. She had almost totally overcome the dread of her own body.

I had never seen anything like it. A middle-aged man, perhaps a salesman, was smoking a cigarette as we came upon him. He took one look at Vida and missed his mouth with the cigarette.

He stood there staring on like a fool, not taking his eyes off Vida, even though her beauty had caused him to lose control of the world.

PSA

THE jet was squat and leering and shark-like with its tail. It was the first time I had ever been on an airplane. It was a strange experience climbing into that thing.

Vida caused her usual panic among the male passengers as we got into our seats. We immediately fastened our seat belts. Everybody who got on the airplane joined the same brotherhood of nervousness.

I looked out the window and we were sitting over

the wing. Then I was surprised to find a rug on the floor of the airplane.

The walls of the airplane had little California scenes on them: cable cars, Hollywood, Coit Tower, the Mount Palomar telescope, a California mission, the Golden Gate Bridge, a zoo, a sailboat, etc. and a building that I couldn't recognize. I looked very hard at the building. Perhaps it was built while I was in the library.

The men continued to stare at Vida, though the airplane was filled with attractive stewardesses. Vida made the stewardesses invisible, which was probably a rare thing for them.

"I really can't believe it," I said.

"They can have it all if they want it. I'm not trying to do anything," Vida said.

"You're really a prize," I said.

"Only because I'm with you," she said.

Before taking off a man talked to us over the plane's PA system. He welcomed us aboard and told us too much about the weather, the temperature, clouds, the sun and the wind and what weather waited for us down California. We didn't want to hear that much about the weather. I hoped he was the pilot.

It was gray and cold outside without any hope for the sun. We were now taking off. We started moving down the runway, slow at first, then faster, faster, faster: my God!

I looked at the wing below me. The rivets in the wing looked awfully gentle as if they were not able to hold anything up. The wing trembled from time to time ever so gently, but just enough to put the subtle point across.

"How does it feel?" Vida said. "You look a little green around the edges."

"It's different," I said.

A medieval flap was hanging down from the wing as we took off. It was the metal intestine of some kind of bird, retractable and visionary.

We flew above the fog clouds and right into the sun. It was fantastic. The clouds were white and beautiful and grew like flowers to the hills and mountains below, hiding with blossoms the valleys from our sight.

I looked down on my wing and saw what looked like a coffee stain as if somebody had put a cup of coffee down on the wing. You could see the ring stain of the cup and then a big splashy sound stain to show that the cup had fallen over.

I was holding Vida's hand.

From time to time we hit invisible things in the air that made the plane buck like a phantom horse.

I looked down at the coffee stain again and I liked it with the world far below. We were going to land at Burbank in Los Angeles in less than an hour to let off and pick up more passengers, then on to San Diego.

We were travelling so fast that it only took a few moments before we were gone.

The Coffee Stain

I WAS beginning to love the coffee stain on my wing. Somehow it was perfect for the day: like a talisman. I started to think about Tijuana, but then I changed my mind and went back to the coffee stain.

Things were going on in the airplane with the stewardesses. They were taking tickets and offering coffee inside the plane, and making themselves generally liked.

The stewardesses were like beautiful *Playboy* nuns coming and going through the corridors of the airplane as if the airplane were a nunnery. They wore short skirts to show off lovely knees, beautiful legs, but their knees and legs became invisible in front of Vida, who sat quietly in her seat next to me, holding my hand, thinking about her body's Tijuana destination.

There was a perfect green pocket in the mountains. It was perhaps a ranch or a field or a pasture. I could have loved that pocket of green forever.

The speed of the airplane made me feel affectionate.

After a while the clouds reluctantly gave up the valleys, but it was a very desolate land we were travelling over, not even the clouds wanted it. There was nothing human kind below, except a few roads that ran like long dry angleworms in the mountains.

Vida remained quiet, beautiful.

The sun kept swinging back and forth on my wing. I looked down beyond my coffee stain to see that we were flying now above a half-desolate valley that showed the agricultural designs of man in yellow and in green. But the mountains had no trees in them and were barren and sloped like ancient surgical instruments.

I looked at the medieval intestinal flap of the wing, rising to digest hundreds of miles an hour, beside my coffee stain talisman.

Vida was perfect, though her eyes were dreaming south.

The people on the other side of the airplane were looking down below at something. I wondered what it was and looked down my side to see a small town and land that looked gentler and there were more towns. The towns began magnifying one another. The gentleness of the land became more and more towns and grew sprawling into Los Angeles and I was looking for a freeway.

The man I hoped was the pilot or involved in some official capacity with the airplane told us that we were going to land in two minutes. We suddenly flew into a cloudy haze that became the Burbank airport. The sun was not shining and everything was murky. It was a yellow murk whereas back in San Francisco it was a gray murk.

The airplane grew empty and then became full again. Vida got a lot of visual action while this was going on. One of the stewardesses lingered for a minute a few seats away and stared at Vida as if to make sure she were really there.

"How do you feel?" I said.

"Fine," Vida said.

A small airliner about the size of a P-38 with rusty-looking propellers taxied by to take off. Its windows were filled with terrified passengers.

Some businessmen were now sitting in front of us. They were talking about a girl. They all wanted to go to bed with her. She was a secretary in a branch office in Phoenix. They were talking about her, using business language. "I'd like to get her account! Ha-ha! Ha-ha! Ha-ha! Ha-ha-ha-ha!"

The "pilot" welcomed the new people aboard and told us too much about the weather again. Nobody wanted to hear what he had to say.

"We'll be landing in San Diego in twenty-one minutes," he said, finishing his weather report.

As we took off from Burbank, a train was running parallel with us across from the airport. We left it behind as if it weren't there and the same with Los Angeles.

We climbed through the heavy yellow haze and then suddenly the sun was shining calmly away on the wing and my coffee stain looked happy like a surfer, but it was only a passing thing.

Bing-Bonging to San Diego

BING-BONG!

The trip to San Diego was done mostly in the clouds. From time to time a bell tone was heard in the airplane. I didn't know what it was about.

Bing-bong!

The stewardesses wanted more tickets and people to like them. The smiles never left their faces. They were smiling even when they weren't smiling.

Bing-bong!

I thought about Foster and the library, then I very rapidly changed the subject in my mind. I didn't want to think about Foster and the library: *grimace*.

Bing-bong!

Then we flew into heavy fog and the plane made funny noises. The noises were fairly solid. I almost thought that we had landed in San Diego and were moving along the runway when a stewardess told us that we *were* going to land shortly, so we were still in the air.

Hmmmmmmmm . . .

Bing-bong!

Hot Water

FROM San Francisco our speed had been amazing. We had gathered hundreds of miles effortlessly, as if guided by lyrical poetry. Suddenly we broke out into the clear to find that we had been over the ocean. I saw white waves below breaking against the shore and there was San Diego. I saw a thing that looked like a melting park and my ears were popping and we were going down.

The airplane stopped and there were many warships anchored across from the airport and they were in a low gray mist that was the color of their bodies.

"You can stop being green now," Vida said.

"Thank you," I said. "I'm new at the tree game. Perhaps it's not my calling."

We got off the airplane with Vida causing her customary confusion among the male passengers and resentment among the female passengers.

Two sailors looked as if their eyes had been jammed with pinball machines and we went on into the terminal. It was small and old-fashioned.

And I had to go to the toilet.

The difference between the San Francisco International Airport and the San Diego International Airport is the men's toilet.

In the San Francisco International Airport the hot water stays on by itself when you wash your hands, but in the San Diego International Airport, it doesn't. You have to hold the spigot all the time you want hot water.

While I was making hot water observations, Vida had five passes made at her. She brushed them off like flies.

I felt like having a drink, a very unusual thing for me, but the bar was small, dark and filled with sailors. I didn't like the looks of the bartender. It didn't look like a good bar.

There was more confusion and distraction among the men in the terminal. One man actually fell down. I don't know how he did it, but he did it. He was lying there on the floor staring up at Vida just as I decided not to have a drink in the bar but a cup of coffee in the cafe instead.

"I think you've affected his inner ear," I said.

"Poor man," Vida said.

Flying Backwards

THE basic theme of the San Diego airport cafe was small and casual with a great many young people and boxes full of wax flowers.

The cafe was also filled with a lot of airplane

folks: stewardesses and pilots and people talking about airplanes and flight.

Vida had her effect on them while I ordered two cups of coffee from a waitress in a white uniform. She was not young or pretty and she was not quite awake either.

The cafe windows were covered with heavy green curtains that held the light out and you couldn't see anything outside, not even a wing.

"Well, here we are," I said.

"That's for certain," Vida said.

"How do you feel?" I said.

"I wish it were over," Vida said.

"Yeah."

There were two men sitting next to us talking about airplanes and the wind and the number eighty kept coming up again and again. They were talking about miles per hour.

"Eighty," one of them said.

I lost track of what they were saying because I was thinking about the abortion in Tijuana and then I heard one of them say, "At eighty you'd actually be flying the plane backwards."

Downtown

It was an overcast nothing day in San Diego. We took a Yellow Cab downtown. The driver was drinking coffee. We got in and he took a long good look at Vida while he finished with his coffee.

"Where to?" he said, more to Vida than to me.

"The Green Hotel," I said. "It's—"

"I know where it's at," he said to Vida.

He drove us onto a freeway.

"Do you think the sun will come out?" I said, not knowing what else to say. Of course I didn't have to say anything, but he was really staring at Vida in his rear-view mirror.

"It will pop out around twelve or so, but I like it this way," he said to Vida.

So I took a good look at his face in the mirror. He looked as if he had been beaten to death with a wine bottle, but by doing it with the contents of the bottle.

"Here we are," he said to Vida, finally pulling up in front of the Green Hotel.

The fare was one dollar and ten cents, so I gave him a twenty-cent tip. This made him very unhappy. He was staring at the money in his hand as we walked away from the cab and into the Green Hotel.

He didn't even say good-bye to Vida.

The Green Hotel

THE Green Hotel was a four-story red brick hotel across the street from a parking lot and next to a bookstore. I couldn't help but look at the books in the window. They were different from the books that we had in the library.

The desk clerk looked up as we came into the hotel. The hotel had a big green plant in the window with enormous leaves.

"Hello, there!" he said. He was very friendly with a lot of false teeth in his mouth.

"Hello," I said.

Vida smiled.

That really pleased him because he became twice as friendly, which was hard to do.

"Foster sent us," I said.

"Oh, Foster!" he said. "Yes. Yes. Foster. He called and said you were coming and here you are! Mr. and Mrs. Smith. Foster. Wonderful person! Foster, yes."

He was really smiling up a storm now. Maybe he was the father of an airline stewardess.

"I have a lovely room with a bath and view," he said. "It's just like home. You'll adore it," he said to Vida. "It's not like a hotel room."

For some reason he did not like the idea of Vida staying in a hotel room, though he ran a hotel, and that was only the beginning.

"Yeah, it's a beautiful room," he said. "Very lovely. It'll help you enjoy your stay in San Diego. How long will you be here? Foster didn't say much over the telephone. He just said you were coming and here you are!"

"Just a day or so," I said.

"Business or pleasure?" he said.

"We're visiting her sister," I said.

"Oh, that sounds nice. She has a small place, huh?"

"I snore," I said.

"Oh," the desk clerk said.

I signed Mr. and Mrs. Smith of San Francisco on the hotel register. Vida watched me as I signed our new instant married name. She was smiling. My! how beautiful she looked.

"I'll show you to your room," the desk clerk said. "It's a beautiful room. You'll be happy in it. The walls are thick, too. You'll be at home."

"Good to hear," I said. "My affliction has caused me a lot of embarrassment in the past."

"Really a loud snorer?" he said.

"Yes," I said. "Like a sawmill."

"If you'll please wait a minute," he said. "I'll ring my brother and have him come down and watch the desk while I'm taking you upstairs to the room."

He pushed a silent buzzer that summoned his brother down the elevator a few moments later.

"Some nice people here. Mr. and Mrs. Smith.

Friends of Foster," the desk clerk said. "I'm going to give them Mother's room."

The brother clerk gave Vida a solid once-over as he went behind the desk to take over the wheel from his brother who stepped out and he stepped in.

They were both middle-aged.

"That's good," the brother desk clerk said, satisfied. "They'll love Mother's room."

"Your mother lives here?" I said, now a little confused.

"No, she's dead," the desk clerk said. "But it was her room before she died. This hotel has been in the family for over fifty years. Mother's room is just the way it was when she died. God bless her. We haven't touched a thing. We only rent it out to nice people like yourselves."

We got into an ancient dinosaur elevator that took us up to the fourth floor and Mother's room. It was a nice room in a dead mother kind of way.

"Beautiful, isn't it?" the desk clerk said.

"Very comfortable," I said.

"Lovely," Vida said.

"You'll enjoy San Diego even more with this room," he said.

He pulled up the window shade to show us an excellent view of the parking lot, which was fairly exciting if you'd never seen a parking lot before.

"I'm sure we will," I said.

"If there's anything you want, just let me know and we'll take care of it: a call in the morning, anything, just let us know. We're here to make your stay in San Diego enjoyable, even if you can't stay at your sister's because you snore."

"Thank you," I said.

He left and we were alone in the room.

"What's the snoring thing you told him about?" Vida said, sitting down on the bed.

She was smiling.

"I don't know," I said. "It just seemed like the proper thing to do."

"You are a caution," Vida said. Then she freshened herself up a little, washed the air travel off and we were ready to go visit Dr. Garcia in Tijuana.

"Well, I guess we'd better go," I said.

"I'm ready," Vida said.

The ghost of the dead mother watched us as we left. She was sitting on the bed knitting a ghost thing.

The Bus to Tijuana

I DON'T like San Diego. We walked the few blocks to the Greyhound bus depot. There were baskets of flowers hanging from the light posts.

There was almost a small town flavor to San Diego that morning except for the up-all-night tired sailors or just-starting-out sailors walking along the streets.

The Greyhound bus depot was jammed with people and games of amusement and vending machines and there were more Mexicans in the bus depot than on the streets of San Diego. It was almost as if the bus depot were the Mexican part of town.

Vida's body, perfect face and long lightning hair performed their customary deeds among the men in the bus depot, causing a thing that was just short of panic.

"Well," I said.

Vida replied with a silence.

The bus to Tijuana left every fifteen minutes and cost sixty cents. There were a lot of Mexican men in the line wearing straw and cowboy hats in sprawled laziness to Tijuana.

A jukebox was playing square pop tunes from the time that I had gone into the library. It was strange to hear those old songs again.

There was a young couple waiting for the bus in front of us. They were very conservative in dress and manner and seemed to be awfully nervous and bothered and trying hard to hold on to their composure.

There was a man standing in the line, holding a racing form under his arm. He was old with dandruff on the lapels and shoulders of his coat and on his racing form.

I had never been to Tijuana before but I had been to a couple of other border towns: Nogales and Juarez. I didn't look forward to Tijuana.

Border towns are not very pleasant places. They bring out the worst in both countries, and everything that is American stands out like a neon sore in border towns.

I noticed the middle-aged people, growing old, that you always see in crowded bus depots but never in empty ones. They exist only in numbers and seem to live in crowded bus depots. They all looked as if they were enjoying the old records on the jukebox.

One Mexican man was carrying a whole mess of stuff in a Hunt's tomato sauce box and in a plastic bread wrapper. They seemed to be his possessions and he was going home with them to Tijuana.

Slides

As we drove the short distance to Tijuana it was not a very pleasant trip. I looked out the window to see that there was no wing on the bus, no coffee stain out there. I missed it.

San Diego grew very poor and then we were on a freeway. The country down that way is pretty nothing and not worth describing.

Vida and I were holding hands. Our hands were together in our hands as our real fate moved closer to us. Vida's stomach was flat and perfect and it was going to remain that way.

Vida looked out the window at what is not worth

describing, but even more so and done in cold cement freeway language. She didn't say anything.

The young conservative couple sat like frozen beans in their seats in front of us. They were really having a bad time of it. I pretty much guessed why they were going to Tijuana.

The man whispered something to the woman. She nodded without saying anything. I thought she was going to start crying. She bit her lower lip.

I looked down from the bus into cars and saw things in the back seats. I tried hard not to look at the people but instead to look at the things in the back seats. I saw a paper bag, three coat hangers, some flowers, a sweater, a coat, an orange, a paper bag, a box, a dog.

"We're on a conveyer belt," Vida said.

"It's easier this way," I said. "It will be all right. Don't worry."

"I know it will be all right," she said. "But I wish we were there. Those people in front of us are worse than the idea of the abortion."

The man started to whisper something to the woman, who continued staring straight ahead, and Vida turned and looked out the window at the nothing leading to Tijuana.

The Man from Guadalajara

THE border was a mass of cars coming and going in excitement and confusion to pass under an heroic arch into Mexico. There was a sign that said something like: WELCOME TO TIJUANA THE MOST VISITED CITY IN THE WORLD.

I had a little trouble with that one.

We just walked across the border into Mexico. The Americans didn't even say good-bye and we were suddenly in a different way of doing things.

First there were Mexican guards wearing those .45 caliber automatic pistols that Mexicans love, checking the cars going into Mexico.

Then there were other men who looked like detectives standing along the pedestrian path to Mexico. They didn't say a word to us, but they stopped two people behind us, a young man and woman, and asked them what nationality they were and they said Italian.

"We're Italians."

I guess Vida and I looked like Americans.

The arch, besides being heroic, was beautiful and modern and had a nice garden with many fine river rocks in the garden, but we were more interested in getting a taxi and went to a place where there were many taxis.

I noticed that famous sweet acrid dust that covers Northern Mexico. It was like meeting a strange old friend again.

"TAXI!"

"TAXI!"

"TAXI!"

The drivers were yelling and motioning a new supply of gringos toward them.

"TAXI!"

"TAXI!"

"TAXI!"

The taxis were typically Mexican and the drivers were shoving them like pieces of meat. I don't like people to try and use the hard sell on me. I'm not made for it.

The conservative young couple came along, looking very frightened, and got into a taxi and disappeared toward Tijuana that lay flat before us and then sloped up into some hazy yellow poor-looking hills with a great many houses on them.

The air was beginning electric with the hustle for the Yankee dollar and its biblical message. The taxi drivers seemed to be endless like flies trying to get you into their meat for Tijuana and its joys.

"Hey, beau-ti-ful girl and BE-atle! Get in!" a driver yelled at us.

"Beatle?" I said to Vida. "Is my hair that long?"

"It is a little long," Vida said, smiling.

"Hey, BE-atle and hey, beauty!" another driver yelled.

There was a constant buzzing of TAXI! TAXI! TAXI! Suddenly everything had become speeded up for us in Mexico. We were now in a different country, a country that just wanted to see our money.

"TAXI!"

"TAXI!"

(Wolf whistle.)

"BE-atle!"

"TAXI!"

"HEY! THERE!"

"TAXI!".

"TIJUANA!"

"SHE'S GOOD-LOOKING!"

"TAXI!"

(Wolf whistle.)

"TAXI!"

"TAXI!"

"SENORITA! SENORITA! SENORITA!"

"HEY, BEATLE! TAXI!"

And then a Mexican man walked quietly up to us. He seemed a little embarrassed. He was wearing a business suit and was about forty years old.

"I have a car," he said. "Would you like a ride downtown? It's right over there."

It was a ten-year-old Buick, dusty, but well kept up and seemed to want us to get into it.

"Thank you," I said. "That would be very nice."

The man looked all right, just wanting to be helpful, so it seemed. He didn't look as if he were selling anything.

"It's right over here," he repeated, to show that the car was something that he took pride in owning.

"Thank you," I said.

We walked over to his car. He opened the door for us and then went around and got in himself.

"It's noisy here," he said, as we started driving the mile or less to Tijuana. "Too much noise."

"It is a little noisy," I said.

After we left the border he kind of relaxed and turned toward us and said, "Did you come across for the afternoon?"

"Yes, we thought we'd take a look at Tijuana while we're visiting her sister in San Diego," I said.

"It's something to look at all right," he said. He didn't look too happy when he said that.

"Do you live here?" I said.

"I was born in Guadalajara," he said. "That's a beautiful city. That's my home. Have you ever been there? It's beautiful."

"Yes," I said. "I was there five or six years ago. It is a lovely city."

I looked out the window to see a small carnival lying abandoned by the road. The carnival was flat and stagnant like a mud puddle.

"Have you ever been to Mexico before, Señora?" he said, fatherly.

"No," Vida said. "This is my first visit."

"Don't judge Mexico by this," he said. "Mexico is different from Tijuana. I've been working here for a year and in a few months I'll go back home to Guadalajara, and I'm going to stay there this time. I was a fool to leave."

"What do you do?" I said.

"I work for the government," he said. "I'm taking

a survey among the Mexican people who come and go across the border into your country."

"Are you finding out anything interesting?" Vida said.

"No," he said. "It's all the same. Nothing is different."

A Telephone Call from Woolworth's

THE government man, whose name we never got, left us on the Main Street of Tijuana and pointed out the Government Tourist Building as a place that could tell us things to do while we were in Tijuana.

The Government Tourist Building was small and glass and very modern and had a statue in front of it. The statue was a gray stone statue and did not look at peace. It was taller than the building. The statue was a pre-Columbian god or fella doing something that did not make him happy.

Though the building was quite attractive, there was nothing the people in that little building could do for us. We needed another service from the Mexican people.

Everybody was shoving us for dollars, trying to sell us things that we didn't want: kids with gum, people wanting us to buy border junk from them, more taxicab drivers shouting that they wanted to take us back to the border, even though we had just gotten there, or to other places where we would have some fun.

"TAXI!"

"BEAUTIFUL GIRL!"

"TAXI!"

"BEATLE!"

(Wolf whistle.)

The taxicab drivers of Tijuana remained constant in their devotion to us. I had no idea my hair was so long and of course Vida had her thing going.

We went over to the big modern Woolworth's on the Main Street of Tijuana to find a telephone. It was a pastel building with a big red Woolworth's sign and a red brick front and big display windows all filled up with Easter stuff: lots and lots and lots of bunnies and yellow chicks bursting happily out of huge eggs.

The Woolworth's was so antiseptic and clean and orderly compared to the outside which was just a few feet away or not away at all if you looked past the bunnies in the front window.

There were very attractive girls working as sales girls, dark and young and doing lots of nice things with their eyes. They all looked as if they should work in a bank instead of Woolworth's.

I asked one of the girls where the telephone was and she pointed out the direction to me.

"It's over there," she said in good-looking English.

I went over to the telephone with Vida spreading erotic confusion like missile jam among the men in the store. The Mexican women, though very pretty, were no match for Vida. She shot them down without even thinking about it.

The telephone was beside an information booth, next to the toilet, near a display of leather belts and a display of yarn and the women's blouse section.

What a bunch of junk to remember, but that's what I remember and look forward to the time I forget it.

The telephone operated on American money: a nickel like it used to be in the good old days of my childhood.

A man answered the telephone.

He sounded like a doctor.

"Hello, Dr. Garcia?" I said.

"Yes."

"A man named Foster called you yesterday about our problem. Well, we're here," I said.

"Good. Where are you?"

"We're at Woolworth's," I said.

"Please excuse my English. Isn't so good. I'll get the girl. Her English is . . . better. She'll tell you how to get here. I'll be waiting. Everything is all right."

A girl took over the telephone. She sounded very young and said, "You're at Woolworth's."

"Yes," I said.

"You're not very far away," she said.

That seemed awfully strange to me.

"When you leave Woolworth's, turn right and walk down three blocks and then turn left on Fourth Street, walk four blocks and then turn left again off Fourth Street," she said. "We are in a green building in the middle of the block. You can't miss it. Did you get that?"

"Yes," I said. "When we leave Woolworth's, we turn right and walk three blocks down to Fourth Street, then we turn left on Fourth Street, and walk four blocks and then turn left again off Fourth Street, and there's a green building in the middle of the block, and that's where you're at."

Vida was listening.

"Your wife hasn't eaten, has she?"

"No," I said.

"Good, we'll be waiting for you. If you should get lost, telephone again."

We left Woolworth's and followed the girl's directions amid being hustled by souvenir junk salesmen, the taxi drivers and gum kids of Tijuana, surrounded by wolf whistles, cars cars cars, and cries of animal consternation and HEY, BEATLE!

Fourth Street had waited eternally for us to come as we were always destined to come, Vida and me, and now we'd come, having started out that morning in San Francisco and our lives many years before.

The streets were filled with cars and people and a fantastic feeling of excitement. The houses did not have any lawns, only that famous dust. They were our guides to Dr. Garcia.

There was a brand-new American car parked in front of the green building. The car had California license plates. I didn't have to think about that one too much to come up with an answer. I looked in the back seat. There was a girl's sweater lying there. It looked helpless.

Some children were playing in front of the doctor's office. The children were poor and wore unhappy clothes. They stopped playing and watched us as we went in.

We were no doubt a common sight for them. They had probably seen many gringos in this part of town, going into this green adobe-like building, gringos who did not look very happy. We did not disappoint them.

BOOK 5:

My Three Abortions

Furniture Studies

THERE was a small bell to ring on the door. It was not like the silver bell of my library, so far away from this place. You rang this bell by pressing your finger against it. That's what I did.

We had to wait a moment for someone to answer. The children stayed away from their play to watch us. The children were small, ill-dressed and dirty. They had those strange undernourished bodies and faces that make it so hard to tell how old children are in Mexico.

A child that looks five will turn out to be eight. A child that looks seven will actually be ten. It's horrible.

Some Mexican mother women came by. They looked at us, too. Their eyes were expressionless, but showed in this way that they knew we were *abortionistas*.

Then the door to the doctor's office opened effortlessly as if it had always planned to open at that time and it was Dr. Garcia himself who opened the door for us. I didn't know what he looked like, but I knew it was him.

"Please," he said, gesturing us in.

"Thank you," I said. "I just called you on the telephone. I'm Foster's friend."

"I know," he said, quietly. "Follow, please."

The doctor was small, middle-aged and dressed perfectly like a doctor. His office was large and cool and had many rooms that led like a labyrinth far into the back and places that we knew nothing about.

He took us to a small reception room. It was clean with modern linoleum on the floor and modern doctor furniture: an uncomfortable couch and three chairs that you could never really fit into.

The furniture was the same as the furniture you see in the offices of American doctors. There was a tall plant in the corner with large flat cold green leaves. The leaves didn't do anything.

There were some other people already in the room: a father, a mother and a young teen-age daughter. She obviously belonged to the brand-new car parked in front.

"Please," the doctor said, gesturing us toward the two empty chairs in the room. "Soon," he said, smiling gently. "Wait, please. Soon."

He went away across the corridor and into another room that we could not see, leaving us with the three people. They were not talking and it was strangely quiet all through the building.

Everybody looked at everybody else in a nervous kind of way that comes when time and circumstance reduce us to seeking illegal operations in Mexico.

The father looked like a small town banker in the San Joaquin Valley and the mother looked like a woman who participated in a lot of social activities.

The daughter was pretty and obviously intelligent and didn't know what to do with her face as she waited for her abortion, so she kept smiling in a rapid knife-like way at nothing.

The father looked very stern as if he were going to refuse a loan and the mother looked vaguely shocked as if somebody had said something a little risqué at a social tea for the Friends of the DeMolay.

The daughter, though she possessed a narrow budding female body, looked as if she were too young to have an abortion. She should have been doing something else.

I looked over at Vida. She also looked as if she were too young to have an abortion. What were we all doing there? Her face was growing pale.

Alas, the innocence of love was merely an escalating physical condition and not a thing shaped like our kisses.

My First Abortion

About forever or ten minutes passed and then the doctor came back and motioned toward Vida and me to come with him, though the other people had been waiting when we came in. Perhaps it had something to do with Foster.

"Please," Dr. Garcia said, quietly.

We followed after him across the hall and into a small office. There was a desk in the office and a typewriter. The office was dark and cool, the shades were down, with a leather chair and photographs of the doctor and his family upon the walls and the desk.

There were various certificates showing the medical degrees the doctor had obtained and what schools he had graduated from.

There was a door that opened directly into an operating room. A teen-age girl was in the room cleaning up and a young boy, another teen-ager, was helping her.

A big blue flash of fire jumped across a tray full of surgical instruments. The boy was sterilizing the instruments with fire. It startled Vida and me. There was a table in the operating room that had metal things to hold your legs and there were leather straps that went with them.

"No pain," the doctor said to Vida and then to me. "No pain and clean, all clean, no pain. Don't worry. No pain and clean. Nothing left. I'm a doctor," he said.

I didn't know what to say. I was so nervous that I was almost in shock. All the color had drained from Vida's face and her eyes looked as if they could not see any more.

"250 dollars," the doctor said. "Please."

"Foster said it would be 200 dollars. That's all we have," I heard my own voice saying. "200. That's what you told Foster."

"200. That's all you have?" the doctor said.

Vida stood there listening to us arbitrate the price of her stomach. Vida's face was like a pale summer cloud.

"Yes," I said. "That's all we have."

I took the money out of my pocket and gave it to the doctor. I held the money out and he took it from my hand. He put it in his pocket, without counting it, and then he became a doctor again, and that's the way he stayed all the rest of the time we were there.

He had only stopped being a doctor for a moment. It was a little strange. I don't know what I expected. It was very good that he stayed a doctor for the rest of the time.

Foster was of course right.

He became a doctor by turning to Vida and smiling and saying, "I won't hurt you and it will be clean. Nothing left after and no pain, honey. Believe me. I'm a doctor."

Vida smiled 1/2: ly.

"How long has she been?" the doctor said to me and starting to point at her stomach but not following through with it, so his hand was a gesture that didn't do anything.

"About five or six weeks," I said.

Vida was now smiling 1/4: ly.

The doctor paused and looked at a calendar in his mind and then he nodded affectionately at the calendar. It was probably a very familiar calendar to him. They were old friends.

"No breakfast?" he said, starting to point again at Vida's stomach but again he failed to do so.

"No breakfast," I said.

"Good girl," the doctor said.

Vida was now smiling 1/37: ly.

After the boy finished sterilizing the surgical instruments, he took a small bucket back through another large room that was fastened to the operating room.

The other room looked as if it had beds in it. I moved my head a different way and I could see a bed in it and there was a girl lying on the bed asleep and there was a man sitting in a chair beside the bed. It looked very quiet in the room.

A moment after the boy left the operating room, I heard a toilet flush and water running from a tap and then the sound of water being poured in the toilet and the toilet was flushed again and the boy came back with the bucket.

The bucket was empty.

The boy had a large gold wristwatch on his hand.

"Everything's all right," the doctor said.

The teen-age girl, who was dark and pretty and also had a nice wristwatch, came into the doctor's office and smiled at Vida. It was that kind of smile that said: It's time now; please come with me.

"No pain, no pain, no pain," the doctor repeated like a nervous nursery rime.

No pain, I thought, how strange.

"Do you want to watch?" the doctor asked me, gesturing toward an examination bed in the operating room where I could sit if I wanted to watch the abortion.

I looked over at Vida. She didn't want me to watch and I didn't want to watch either.

"No," I said. "I'll stay in here."

"Please come, honey," the doctor said.

The girl touched Vida's arm and Vida went into the operating room with her and the doctor closed the door, but it didn't really close. It was still open an inch or so.

"This won't hurt," the girl said to Vida. She was giving Vida a shot.

Then the doctor said something in Spanish to the boy who said OK and did something.

"Take off your clothes," the girl said. "And put this on."

Then the doctor said something in Spanish and the boy answered him in Spanish and the girl said, "Please. Now put your legs up. That's it. Good. Thank you."

"That's right, honey," the doctor said. "That didn't hurt, did it? Everything's going to be all right. You're a good girl."

Then he said something to the boy in Spanish and then the girl said something in Spanish to the doctor who said something in Spanish to both of them.

Everything was very quiet for a moment or so in the operating room. I felt the dark cool of the doctor's office on my body like the hand of some other kind of doctor.

"Honey?" the doctor said. "Honey?"

There was no reply.

Then the doctor said something in Spanish to the boy and the boy answered him in something metallic, surgical. The doctor used the thing that was metallic and surgical and gave it back to the boy who gave him something else that was metallic and surgical.

Everything was either quiet or metallic and surgical in there for a while.

Then the girl said something in Spanish to the boy who replied to her in English. "I know," he said.

The doctor said something in Spanish.

The girl answered him in Spanish.

A few moments passed during which there were no more surgical sounds in the room. There was now the sound of cleaning up and the doctor and the girl and the boy talked in Spanish as they finished up.

Their Spanish was not surgical any more. It was just casual cleaning-up Spanish.

"What time is it?" the girl said. She didn't want to look at her watch.

"Around one," the boy said.

The doctor joined them in English. "How many more?" he said.

"Two," the girl said.

"¿Dos?" the doctor said in Spanish.

"There's one coming," the girl said.

The doctor said something in Spanish.

The girl answered him in Spanish.

"I wish it was three," the boy said in English.

"Stop thinking about girls," the doctor said, jokingly.

Then the doctor and the girl were involved in a brief very rapid conversation in Spanish.

This was followed by a noisy silence and then the sound of the doctor carrying something heavy and unconscious out of the operating room. He put the thing down in the other room and came back a moment later.

The girl walked over to the door of the room I was in and finished opening it. My dark cool office was suddenly flooded with operating room light. The boy was cleaning up.

"Hello," the girl said, smiling. "Please come with me."

She casually beckoned me through the operating room as if it were a garden of roses. The doctor was sterilizing his surgical instruments with the blue flame.

He looked up at me from the burning instruments and said, "Everything went OK. I promised no pain, all clean. The usual." He smiled. "Perfect."

The girl took me into the other room where Vida was lying unconscious on the bed. She had warm covers over her. She looked as if she were dreaming in another century.

"It was an excellent operation," the girl said. "There were no complications and it went as smoothly as possible. She'll wake up in a little while. She's beautiful, isn't she?"

"Yes."

The girl got me a chair and put it down beside Vida. I sat down in the chair and looked at Vida. She was so alone there in the bed. I reached over and touched her cheek. It felt as if it had just come unconscious from an operating room.

The room had a small gas heater that was burning quietly away in its own time. The room had two beds in it and the other bed where the girl had lain a short while before was now empty and there was an empty chair beside the bed, as this bed would be empty soon and the chair I was now sitting in: to be empty.

The door to the operating room was open, but I couldn't see the operating table from where I was sitting.

My Second Abortion

THE door to the operating room was open, but I couldn't see the operating table from where I was sitting. A moment later they brought in the teen-age girl from the waiting room.

"Everything's going to be all right, honey," the doctor said. "This won't hurt." He gave her the shot himself.

"Please take off your clothes," the girl said.

There was a stunned silence for a few seconds that bled into the awkward embarrassed sound of the teenage girl taking her clothes off.

After she took off her clothes, the girl assistant who was no older than the girl herself said, "Put this on."

The girl put it on.

I looked down at the sleeping form of Vida. She was wearing one, too.

Vida's clothes were folded over a chair and her shoes were on the floor beside the chair. They looked very sad because she had no power over them any more. She lay unconscious before them.

"Now put your legs up, honey," the doctor was saying. "A little higher, please. That's a good girl."

Then he said something in Spanish to the Mexican girl and she answered him in Spanish.

"I've had six months of Spanish I in high school," the teen-age girl said with her legs apart and strapped to the metal stirrups of this horse of no children.

The doctor said something in Spanish to the Mexican girl and she replied in Spanish to him.

"Oh," he said, a little absentmindedly to nobody in particular. I guess he had performed a lot of abortions that day and then he said to the teen-age girl, "That's nice. Learn some more."

The boy said something very rapidly in Spanish.

The Mexican girl said something very rapidly in Spanish.

The doctor said something very rapidly in Spanish and then he said to the teen-age girl, "How do you feel, honey?"

"Nothing," she said, smiling. "I don't feel anything. Should I feel something right now?"

The doctor said something very rapidly to the boy in Spanish. The boy did not reply.

"I want you to relax," the doctor said to the teen-age girl. "Please take it easy."

All three of them had a very rapid go at it in

Spanish. There seemed to be some trouble and then the doctor said something very rapidly in Spanish to the Mexican girl. He finished it by saying, "¿Como se dice treinta?"

"Thirty," the Mexican girl said.

"Honey," the doctor said. He was leaning over the teen-age girl. "I want you to count to, to thirty for us, please, honey."

"All right," she said, smiling, but for the first time her voice sounded a little tired.

It was starting to work.

"1, 2, 3, 4, 5, 6 . . ." There was a pause here. "7, 8, 9 . . ." There was another pause here, but it was a little longer than the first pause.

"Count to, to thirty, honey," the doctor said.

"10, 11, 12."

There was a total stop.

"Count to thirty, honey," the boy said. His voice sounded soft and gentle just like the doctor's. Their voices were the sides of the same coin.

"What comes after 12?" the teen-age girl giggled. "I know! 13." She was very happy that 13 came after 12. "14, 15, 15, 15."

"You said 15," the doctor said.

"15," the teen-age girl said.

"What's next, honey?" the boy said.

"15," the teen-age girl said very slowly and triumphantly.

"What's next, honey?" the doctor said.

"15," the girl said. "15."

"Come on, honey," the doctor said.

"What's next?" the boy said.

"What's next?" the doctor said.

The girl didn't say anything.

They didn't say anything either. It was very quiet in the room. I looked down at Vida. She was very quiet, too.

Suddenly the silence in the operating room was broken by the Mexican girl saying, "16."

"What?" the doctor said.

"Nothing," the Mexican girl said, and then the language and silences of the abortion began.

Chalkboard Studies

VIDA lay there gentle and still like marble dust on the bed. She had not shown the slightest sign of consciousness, but I wasn't worried because her breathing was normal.

So I just sat there listening to the abortion going on in the other room and looking at Vida and where I was at: this house in Mexico, so far away from my San Francisco library.

The small gas heater was doing its thing because it was cool within the adobe walls of the doctor's office.

Our room was in the center of a labyrinth.

There was a little hall on one side of the room,

running back past the open door of the toilet and ending at a kitchen.

The kitchen was about twenty feet away from where Vida lay unconscious with her stomach vacant like a chalkboard. I could see the refrigerator and a sink in the kitchen and a stove with some pans on it.

On the other side of our room was a door that led into a huge room, almost like a small gym, and I could see still another room off the gym.

The door was open and there was the dark abstraction of another bed in the room like a large flat sleeping animal.

I looked down at Vida still submerged in a vacuum of anesthesia and listened to the abortion ending in the operating room.

Suddenly there was a gentle symphonic crash of surgical instruments and then I could hear the sounds of cleaning up joined to another chalkboard.

My Third Abortion

THE doctor came through the room carrying the teenage girl in his arms. Though the doctor was a small man, he was very strong and carried the girl without difficulty.

She looked very silent and unconscious. Her hair hung strangely over his arm in a blond confusion. He took the girl through the small gym and into the adjoining room where he lay her upon the dark animal-like bed.

Then he came over and closed the door to our room and went into the forward reaches of the labyrinth and came back with the girl's parents.

"It went perfect," he said. "No pain, all clean."

They didn't say anything to him and he came back to our room. As he passed through the door, the people were watching him and they saw Vida lying there and me sitting beside her.

I looked at them and they looked at me before the door was closed. Their faces were a stark and frozen landscape.

The boy came into the room carrying the bucket and he went into the toilet and flushed the fetus and the abortion leftovers down the toilet.

Just after the toilet flushed, I heard the flash of the instruments being sterilized by fire.

It was the ancient ritual of fire and water all over again to be all over again and again in Mexico today.

Vida still lay there unconscious. The Mexican girl came in and looked at Vida. "She's sleeping," the girl said. "It went fine."

She went back into the operating room and then the next woman came into the operating room. She was the "one" coming the Mexican girl had mentioned earlier. I didn't know what she looked like because she had come since we'd been there.

"Has she eaten today?" the doctor said.

"No," a man said sternly, as if he were talking about dropping a hydrogen bomb on somebody he didn't like.

The man was her husband. He had come into the operating room. He had decided that he wanted to watch the abortion. They were awfully tense people and the woman said only three words all the time she was there. After she had her shot, he helped her off with her clothes.

He sat down while her legs were strapped apart on the operating table. She was unconscious just about the time they finished putting her in position for the abortion because they started almost immediately.

This abortion was done automatically like a machine. There was very little conversation between the doctor and his helpers.

I could feel the presence of the man in the operating room. He was like some kind of statue sitting there looking on, waiting for a museum to snatch him and his wife up. I never saw the woman.

After the abortion the doctor was tired and Vida was still lying there unconscious. The doctor came into the room. He looked down at Vida.

"Not yet," he said, answering his own question.

I said no because I didn't have anything else to do with my mouth.

"It's OK," he said. "Sometimes it's like this."

The doctor looked like an awfully tired man. God only knows how many abortions he had performed that day.

He came over and sat down on the bed. He took Vida's hand and he felt her pulse. He reached down and opened one of her eyes. Her eye looked back at him from a thousand miles away.

"It's all right," he said. "She'll be back in a few moments."

He went into the toilet and washed his hands. After he finished washing his hands, the boy came in with the bucket and took care of that.

The girl was cleaning up in the operating room. The doctor had put the woman on the examination bed in the operating room.

He had quite a thing going just taking care of the bodies.

"OHHHHHHHHHHH!" I heard a voice come from behind the gym door where the doctor had taken the teen-age girl. "OHHHHHHHHHHH!" It was a sentimental drunken voice. It was the girl. "OHHHHHHHHHHH!

"16!" she said. "I-OHHHHHHHHHHH!"

Her parents were talking to her in serious, hushed tones. They were awfully respectable.

"OHHHHHHHHHHHHHHHHHHHHHHHH!"

They were acting as if she had gotten drunk at a family reunion and they were trying to cover up her drunkenness.

"OHHHHHHHHHHH! I feel funny!"

There was total silence from the couple in the operating room. The only sound was the Mexican girl. The boy had come back through our room and had gone somewhere else in the building. He never came back.

After the girl finished cleaning up the operating room, she went into the kitchen and started cooking a big steak for the doctor.

She got a bottle of Miller's beer out of the refrigerator and poured the doctor a big glass of it. He sat down in the kitchen. I could barely see him drinking the beer.

Then Vida started stirring in her sleep. She opened her eyes. They didn't see anything for a moment or so and then they saw me.

"Hi," she said in a distant voice.

"Hi," I said, smiling.

"I feel dizzy," she said, coming in closer.

"Don't worry about it," I said. "Everything is fine."

"Oh, that's good," she said. There.

"Just lie quietly and take it easy," I said.

The doctor got up from the table in the kitchen and came in. He was holding the glass of beer in his hand.

"She's coming back," he said.

"Yes," I said.

"Good," he said. "Good."

He took his glass of beer and went back into the kitchen and sat down again. He was very tired.

Then I heard the people in the outside gym room dressing their daughter. They were in a hurry to leave. They sounded as if they were dressing a drunk.

"I can't get my hands up," the girl said.

Her parents said something stern to her and she got her hands up in the air, but they had so much trouble putting her little brassiere on that they finally abandoned trying and the mother put the brassiere in her purse.

"OHHHHHHHHHH! I'm so dizzy," the girl said as her parents half-carried her, half-dragged her out of the place.

I heard a couple of doors close and then everything was silent, except for the doctor's lunch cooking in the kitchen. The steak was being fried in a very hot pan and it made a lot of noise.

"What's that?" Vida said. I didn't know if she was talking about the noise of the girl leaving or the sound of the steak cooking.

"It's the doctor having lunch," I said.

"Is it that late?" she said.

"Yes," I said.

"I've been out a long time," she said.

"Yes," I said. "We're going to have to leave soon but we won't leave until you feel like it."

"I'll see what I can do," Vida said.

The doctor came back into the room. He was nervous because he was hungry and tired and wanted to close the place up for a while, so he could take it easy, rest some.

Vida looked up at him and he smiled and said, "See, no pain, honey. Everything wonderful. Good girl."

Vida smiled very weakly and the doctor returned to the kitchen and his steak that was ready now.

While the doctor had his lunch, Vida slowly sat up and I helped her get dressed. She tried standing up but it was too hard, so I had her sit back down for a few moments.

While she sat there, she combed her hair and then she tried standing up again but she still didn't have it and sat back down on the bed again.

"I'm still a little rocky," Vida said.

"That's all right."

The woman in the other room had come to and her husband was dressing her almost instantly, saying, "Here. Here. Here. Here," in a painful Okie accent.

"I'm tired," the woman said, using up 2/3 of her vocabulary.

"Here," the man said, helping her put something else on.

After he got her dressed he came into our room and stood there looking for the doctor. He was very embarrassed when he saw Vida sitting on the bed, combing her hair.

"Doctor?" he said.

The doctor got up from his steak and stood in the doorway of the kitchen. The man started to walk toward the door, but then stopped after taking only a few steps.

The doctor came into our room.

"Yes," he said.

"I can't remember where I parked my car," the man said. "Can you call me a taxi?"

"You lost your auto?" the doctor said.

"I parked it next to Woolworth's, but I can't remember where Woolworth's is," the man said. "I can find Woolworth's if I can get downtown. I don't know where to go."

"The boy's coming back," the doctor said. "He'll take you there in his auto."

"Thank you," the man said, returning to his wife in the other room. "Did you hear that?" he said to her.

"Yes," she said, using it all up.

"We'll wait," he said.

Vida looked over at me and I smiled at her and took her hand to my mouth and kissed it.

"Let's try again," she said.

"All right," I said.

She tried it again and this time it was all right. She stood there for a few moments and then said, "I've got it. Let's go."

"Are you sure you have it?" I said.

"Yes."

I helped Vida on with her sweater. The doctor looked at us from the kitchen. He smiled but he didn't say anything. He had done what he was supposed to do and now we did what we were supposed to do. We left.

We wandered out of the room into the gym and worked our way to the front of the place, passing through layers of coolness to the door.

Even though it had remained a gray overcast day, we were stunned by the light and everything was instantly noisy, car-like, confused, poor, rundown and Mexican.

It was as if we had been in a time capsule and now were released again to be in the world.

The children were still playing in front of the doctor's office and again they stopped their games of life to watch two squint-eyed gringos holding, clinging, holding to each other walk up the street and into a world without them.

BOOK 6:

The Hero

Woolworth's Again

We slowly, carefully and abortively made our way back to downtown Tijuana surrounded and bombarded by people trying to sell us things that we did not want to buy.

We had already gotten what we'd come to Tijuana for. I had my arm around Vida. She was all right but she was a little weak.

"How do you feel, honey?" I said.

"I feel all right," she said. "But I'm a little weak."

We saw an old man crouching like a small gum-like piece of death beside an old dilapidated filling station.

"HEY, a pretty, pretty girl!"

Mexican men kept reacting to Vida's now pale beauty.

Vida smiled faintly at me as a taxicab driver dramatically stopped his cab in front of us and leaned out the window and gave a gigantic wolf whistle and said, "WOW! You need a taxi, honey!"

We made our way to the Main Street of Tijuana and found ourselves in front of Woolworth's again and the bunnies in the window.

"I'm hungry," Vida said. She was tired. "So hungry."

"You need something to eat," I said. "Let's go inside and see if we can get you some soup."

"That would be good," she said. "I need something."

We went off the confused dirty Main Street of Tijuana into the clean modern incongruity of Woolworth's. A very pretty Mexican girl took our order at the counter. She asked us what we wanted.

"What would you like?" she said.

"She'd like some soup," I said. "Some clam chowder."

"Yes," Vida said.

"What would you like?" the waitress said in very good Woolworth's English.

"I guess a banana split," I said.

I held Vida's hand while the waitress got our orders. She leaned her head against my shoulder. Then she smiled and said, "You're looking at the future biggest fan The Pill ever had."

"How do you feel?" I said.

"Just like I've had an abortion."

Then the waitress brought us our food. While Vida slowly worked her soup, I worked my banana split. It was the first banana split I'd had in years.

It was unusual fare for the day, but it was no different from anything else that had happened since we'd come to the Kingdom of Tijuana to avail ourselves of the local recreational facilities.

The taxicab driver never took his eyes off Vida as we drove back to America. His eyes looked at us from the rear-view mirror as if he had another face and it was a mirror.

"Did you have a good time in Tijuana?" he said.
"Lovely," I said.
"What did you do?" he said.
"We had an abortion," I said.

"HAHAHAHAHAHAHAVERYFUNNYJOKE!"
the driver laughed.
Vida smiled.
Farewell, Tijuana.
Kingdom of Fire and Water.

The Green Hotel Again

OUR desk clerk was waiting for us, agog with smiles and questions. I had an idea that he drank on the job. There was something about how friendly he was.

"Did you see your sister?" he asked Vida with a big falseteeth smile.

"What?" Vida said. She was tired.

"Yes, we saw her," I said. "She was just as we remembered her."

"Even more so," Vida said, catching the game by the tail.

"That's good," the clerk said. "People should never change. They should always be the same. They are happier that way."

I tried that one on for size and was able to hold a straight face. It had been a long day.

"My wife's a little tired," I said. "I think we'll go up to our room."

"Relatives can be tiring. The excitement of it all. Renewing family ties," the desk clerk said.

"Yes," I said.

He gave us the key to his mother's room.

"I can take you up to the room if you don't remember the way," he said.

"No, that's not necessary," I said. "I remember the way." I headed him off by saying, "It's such a beautiful room."

"Isn't it?" he said.

"Very lovely room," Vida said.

"My mother was so happy there," he said.

We took the old elevator upstairs and I opened the door with the key. "Get off the bed," I said as we went into the room. "Off," I repeated.

"What?" Vida said.

"The Mother Ghost," I said.

"Oh."

Vida lay down on the bed and closed her eyes. I took her shoes off, so she could be more comfortable.

"How do you feel?" I said.

"A little tired."

"Let's take a nap," I said, putting her under the covers and joining her.

We slept for an hour or so and then I woke up. The Mother Ghost was brushing her teeth and I told her to get into the closet until we were gone. She got into the closet and closed the door after her.

"Hey, baby," I said. Vida stirred in her sleep and then opened her eyes.

"What time is it?" she said.

"About the middle of the afternoon," I said.

"What time does our plane leave?" she said.

"6:25," I said. "Do you feel you can make it? If you don't, we'll spend the night here."

"No, I'm all right," she said. "Let's go back to San Francisco. I don't like San Diego. I want to get out of here and leave all this behind."

We got up and Vida washed her face and straightened herself up and felt a lot better, though she was still a little weak.

I told the hotel ghost mother good-bye in the closet and Vida joined me. "Good-bye, ghost," she said.

We went down the elevator to the waiting desk clerk whom I suspected of drinking on the job.

He was startled to see me standing there holding the KLM bag in my hand and returning the room key to him.

"You're not spending the night?" he said.

"No," I said. "We've decided to stay with her sister."

"What about your snoring?" he said.

"I'm going to see a doctor about it," I said. "I can't hide from this all my life. I can't go on living like this forever. I've decided to face it like a man."

Vida gave me a little nudge with her eyes to tell me that I was carrying it a little too far, so I retreated by saying, "You have a lovely hotel here and I'll recommend it to all my friends when they visit San Diego. What do I owe you?"

"Thank you," he said. "Nothing. You're Foster's friend. But you didn't even spend the night."

"That's all right," I said. "You've been very friendly. Thank you and good-bye."

"Good-bye," the desk clerk said. "Come again when you can spend the night."

"We will," I said.

"Good-bye," Vida said.

Suddenly he got a little desperate and paranoid. "There was nothing wrong with the room, was there?" he said. "It was my mother's room."

"Nothing," I said. "It was perfect."

"A wonderful hotel," Vida said. "A beautiful room. A truly beautiful room."

Vida seemed to have calmed him down because he said to us as we were going out the door, "Say hello to your sister for me."

That gave us something to think about as we drove out to the San Diego airport sitting very close together in the back seat of a cab where the driver, American this time, did not take his eyes off Vida in the mirror.

When we first got into the cab, the driver said, "Where to?"

I thought it would be fairly simple just to say, "The International Airport, please."

It wasn't.

"That's the San Diego International Airport, isn't it? That's where you want to go, huh?"

"Yes," I said, knowing that something was wrong.

"I just wanted to be sure," he said. "Because I had a fare yesterday that wanted to go to the International Airport, but it was the Los Angeles International Airport he wanted to go to. That's why I was checking."

Oh, yeah.

"Did you take him?" I said. I didn't have anything else to do and my relationship with the cab driver was obviously out of control.

"Yes," he said.

"He was probably afraid of flying," I said.

The cab driver didn't get the joke because he was watching Vida in the rear-view mirror and Vida was watching me after that one.

The driver continued staring at Vida. He paid very little attention to his driving. It was obviously dangerous to ride in a cab with Vida.

I made a mental note of it for the future, not to have Vida's beauty risk our lives.

The San Diego (Not Los Angeles) International Tipping Abyss

UNFORTUNATELY, the cab driver was very unhappy with the tip I gave him. The fare was again one dollar and ten cents and remindful of the experience we'd had earlier in the day with that first cab driver, I raised the tip-ante to thirty cents.

He was startled by the thirty-cent tip and didn't want to have anything else to do with us. Even Vida didn't make any difference when he saw that thirty cents.

What *is* the tip to the San Diego airport?

Our plane didn't leave for an hour. Vida was quite hungry, so we had something to eat in the cafe. It was about 5:30.

We had hamburgers. It was the first time I'd had a hamburger in years, but it turned out not to be very good. It was flat.

Vida said her hamburger was good, though.

"You've forgotten how a hamburger is supposed to taste," Vida said. "Too many years in the monastery have destroyed your better judgment."

There were two women sitting nearby. One of them had platinum hair and a mink coat. She was middle-aged and talking to a young, blandly pretty girl who was talking in turn about her wedding and the little caps that were being designed for the bridesmaids.

The girl was nice in the leg department but a little short in the titty line or was I spoiled? They departed their table without leaving a tip.

This made the waitress mad.

She was probably a close relative to the two cab drivers I'd met that day in San Diego.

She stared at the tipless table as if it were a sex criminal. Perhaps she was their mother.

Farewell, San Diego

I TOOK a closer look at the San Diego airport. It was petite, uncomplicated with no *Playboy* stuff at all. The people were there to work, not to look pretty.

There was a sign that said something like: Animals arriving as baggage may be claimed in the airline air freight areas in the rear of bldg.

You can bet your life that you don't see signs like that in the San Francisco International Airport.

A young man with crutches, accompanied by three old men, came along as we were going out to wait for our airplane. They all stared at Vida and the young man stared the hardest.

It was a long way from the beautiful PSA preflight lounge in San Francisco to just standing outside, beside a wire fence in San Diego, waiting to get on our airplane that was shark-like and making a high whistling steam sound, wanting very much to fly.

The evening was cold and gray coming down upon us with some palm trees, nearby, by the highway. The palm trees somehow made it seem colder than it actually was. They seemed out of place in the cold.

There was a military band playing beside one of the airplanes parked on the field, but it was too far away to see why they were playing. Maybe some big wig was coming or going. They sounded like my hamburger.

My Secret Talisman Forever

WE got our old seats back over the wing and I was sitting again next to the window. Suddenly it was dark in twelve seconds. Vida was quiet, tired. There was a little light on the end of the wing. I became quite fond of it out there in the dark like a lighthouse burning twenty-three miles away and I made it my secret talisman forever.

A young priest was sitting across the aisle from us. He was quite smitten by Vida for the short distance to Los Angeles.

At first he tried not to be obvious about it, but after a while he surrendered himself to it and one time he leaned across the aisle and was going to say something to Vida. He was actually going to say something to her, but then he changed his mind.

I will probably go on for a long time wondering what he would have said to my poor aborted darling who, though weak and tired from the ways of Tijuana, was the prettiest thing going in the sky above California, the rapidly moving sky to Los Angeles.

I went from the priest's interest in Vida to wondering about Foster at the library, how he was handling the books that were coming in that day.

I hoped he was welcoming them the right way and making the authors feel comfortable and wanted as I made them feel.

"Well, we'll be home soon," Vida said to me after a long silence that was noisy with thought. The priest's composure vibrated with tension when Vida spoke.

"Yes," I said. "I was just thinking about that."

"I know," she said. "I could hear the noise in your mind. I think everything's all right at the library. Foster's doing a good job."

"You're doing a good job yourself," I said.

"Thank you," she said. "It will be good to get home. Back to the library and some sleep."

I was very pleased that she considered the library her home. I looked out the window at my talisman. I loved it as much as the coffee stain flying down.

Perhaps and Eleven

THINGS are different at night. The houses and towns far below demand their beauty and get it in distant lights twinkling with incredible passion. Landing at Los Angeles was like landing inside a diamond ring.

The priest didn't want to get off the plane at Los

Angeles, but he had to because that's where he was going. Perhaps Vida reminded him of somebody. Perhaps his mother was very beautiful and he didn't know how to handle it and that's what drove him to the Cloth and now to see that beauty again in Vida was like swirling back through the mirrors of time.

Perhaps he was thinking about something completely different from what I have ever thought about in my life and his thoughts were of the highest nature and should have been made into a statue . . . perhaps. To quote Foster, "Too many perhapses in the world and not enough people."

I was suddenly wondering about my library again and missed the actual departure of the priest to become part of Los Angeles, to add his share to its size and to take memories of Vida into whatever.

"Did you see that?" Vida said.

"Yes," I said.

"This has been happening ever since I was eleven," she said.

Fresno, Then 3½ Minutes to Salinas

THE stewardesses on this flight were fantastically shallow and had been born from half a woman into a world that possessed absolutely no character except chrome smiles. All of them were of course beautiful.

One of them was pushing a little cart down the aisle, trying to sell us cocktails. She had a singsong inhuman voice that I'm positive was prerecorded by a computer.

"Purchase a cocktail.

"Purchase a cocktail.

"Purchase a cocktail."

While pushing her little cart down the sky.

"Purchase a cocktail.

"Purchase a cocktail.

"Purchase a cocktail."

There were no lights below.

Shine on, O talisman!

I pushed my face against the window and looked very hard and saw a star and I made a wish but I won't tell. Why should I? Purchase a cocktail from pretty Miss Zero and find your own star. There's one for everyone in the evening sky.

There were two women behind us talking about nail polish for the thirty-nine minute way to San Francisco. One of them thought that fingernails without polish should be put under rocks.

Vida had no polish on her fingernails but she didn't care and gave the women's conversation no attention.

From time to time the airplane was bucked by an invisible horse in the sky but it didn't bother me because I was falling in love with the 727 jet, my sky home, my air love.

The pilot or some male voice told us that if we looked out the window, we could see the lights of

Fresno and were 3½ minutes away from the lights of Salinas.

I was already looking for Salinas, but something happened on the plane. One of the women spilt her fingernail polish on a cat ten years ago and I looked away for a moment to wonder about that and missed Salinas, so I pretended my talisman was Salinas.

The Saint of Abortion

We were about to land at San Francisco when the women behind us finished their conversation about fingernail polish.

"I wouldn't be caught dead without fingernail polish," one of them said.

"You're right," the other one said.

We were only three miles away from landing and I couldn't see the wing that led like a black highway to my talisman. It seemed as if we were going to land without a wing, only a talisman.

Ah, the wing appeared magically just as we touched the ground.

There were soldiers everywhere in the terminal. It was as if an army were encamped there. They flipped when they saw Vida. She was increasing the United States Army sperm count by about three tons as we walked through the place, heading toward the van in the parking lot.

Vida also affected the civilian population by causing a man who looked like a banker to walk directly into an Oriental woman, knocking the woman down. She was rather surprised because she had just flown in from Saigon and didn't expect this to happen on her first visit to America.

Alas, another victim of Vida's thing.

"Do you think you can take it?" Vida said.

"We ought to bottle what you've got," I said.

"Vida Pop," Vida said.

"How do you feel?" I said with my arm around her.

"Glad to be home," she said.

Even though the San Francisco International Airport acted like a *Playboy* cybernetic palace wanting to do things for us that we were not quite ready to have done, at that moment I felt that the International Airport was our first home back from Tijuana.

I was also anxious to get back to the library and see Foster.

The Bufano statue waited for us with a peace that we couldn't understand with its strange people fastened projectile-like upon a huge bullet.

As we got into the van, I thought there should be a statue for the Saint of Abortion, whoever that was, somewhere in the parking lot for the thousands of women who had made the same trip Vida and I had just finished, flying into the Kingdom of Fire and Water, the waiting and counting hands of Dr. Garcia and his associates in Mexico.

Thank God, the van had an intimate, relaxed human feeling to it. The van reflected Foster in its smells and ways of life. It felt very good to be in the van after having travelled the story of California.

I put my hand on Vida's lap and that's where it stayed following the red lights of cars in front of us shining back like roses into San Francisco.

A New Life

WHEN we arrived back at the library the first thing we saw was Foster sitting out on the steps in his traditional T-shirt, even though it was now dark and cold.

The lights were on in the library and I wondered what Foster was doing sitting outside on the steps. That didn't seem to be the correct way to run a library.

Foster stood up and waved that big friendly wave of his.

"Hello, there, strangers," he said. "How did it go?"

"Fine," I said, getting out of the van. "What are you doing out here?"

"How's my baby?" Foster said to Vida.

"Great," she said.

"Why aren't you inside?" I said.

"Tired, honey?" Foster said to Vida. He put his arm gently around her.

"A little," she said.

"Well, that's the way it should be, but it won't last long."

"The library?" I said.

"Good girl," Foster said to Vida. "Am I glad to see you! You look like a million dollars in small change. What a sight!" giving her a kiss on the cheek.

"The library?" I said.

Foster turned toward me. "I'm sorry about that," he said, then turning to Vida, "Oh, what a girl!"

"You're sorry about what?" I said.

"Don't worry," Foster said. "It's for the best. You need a rest, a change of scene. You'll be a lot happier now."

"Happier, what? What's going on?"

"Well," Foster said. He had his arm around Vida and she was looking up at him as he tried to explain what was going on.

There was a slight smile on her face that grew larger and larger as Foster continued, "Well, it happened this way. I was sitting there minding your asylum when this lady came in with a book and she—"

I looked away from Foster toward the library where its friendly light was shining out and I looked inside the glass door and I could see a woman sitting behind the desk.

I couldn't see her face but I could see that it was a woman and her form looked quite at home. My heart and my stomach started doing funny things in my body.

"You mean?" I said, unable to find the words.

"That's right," Foster said. "She said the way that I was handling the library was a disgrace and I was a slob and she would take it over now: thank you.

"I told her that you'd been here for years and that you were great with the library and I was just watching it during an emergency. She said that didn't make any difference, that if you had turned the library over to me, even for a day, you didn't deserve to be in charge of the library any more.

"I told her that I worked at the caves and she said that I didn't work there any more, that her brother would take care of it from now on, that I should think of doing something else like getting a job.

"Then she asked me where the living quarters were and I pointed out the way and she went in and packed all your stuff. When she found Vida's things there, she said, 'I got here just in time!' Then she had me take it all out here and I've been sitting here ever since."

I looked down at my meager possessions piled on the steps. I hadn't even noticed them.

"I can't believe it," I said. "I'll go tell her that it's all a mistake, that—"

Just then the woman got up from behind the desk and strolled very aggressively to the front door and opened the door without stepping outside and she yelled at me, "Get your God-damn stuff out of here right now and never come back, not unless you've got a book under your arm!"

"There's been a mistake," I said.

"Yes," she said. "I know and you are it. Farewell, creep!"

She turned and the front door closed behind her as if it were obeying her.

I stood there like Lot's wife on one of her bad days.

Vida was laughing like hell and Foster was, too. They started doing a little dance on the sidewalk around me.

"There must be a mistake," I cried in the wilderness.

"You heard the lady," Foster said. "Damn! Damn! Damn! am I glad to be out of the cave business. I thought I was going to get TB."

"Oh, darling," Vida said, breaking the dance to throw her arms around me while Foster started loading our stuff into the van. "You've just been fired. You're going to have to live like a normal human being."

"I can't believe it," I sighed. Then they loaded me into the van.

"Well, what are we going to do?" Foster said.

"Let's go to my place," Vida said. "It's just around the block on Lyon Street."

"I can always sleep in the van," Foster said.

"No, there's plenty of room in my place for all of us," Vida said.

Somehow Vida had ended up driving the van and she parked it in front of a big red shingled house that had an ancient iron fence in front of it. The fench looked quite harmless. Time had removed its ferocity and Vida lived in the attic.

Her place was nice and simple. There was practically no furniture and the walls were painted white and there was nothing on them.

We sat on the floor on a thick white rug that had a low marble table in the center of it.

"Do you want a drink?" Vida said. "I think we all need a drink."

Foster smiled.

She made us some very dry vodka martinis in glasses full of ice. She didn't put any vermouth in them. The drinks were done off with twists of lemon peel. The lemon lay there like flowers in the ice.

"I'll put something on the stereo," Vida said. "Then I'll start some dinner."

I was shocked by losing my library and surprised at being inside a real house again. Both feelings were passing like ships in the night.

"Damn, does that vodka taste good!" Foster said.

"No, honey," I said. "I think you'd better rest. I'll cook up something."

"No," Foster said. "A little logger breakfast is what we all need now. Some fried potatoes and onions and eggs all cooked together with a gallon of catsup on top. Do you have the makings?"

"No," Vida said. "But there's a store open down at California and Divisadero."

"OK," Foster said.

He put some more vodka in his mouth.

"Ah, do you kids have any money left? I'm flat."

I gave Foster a couple of dollars that I had left and he went to the store.

Vida put a record on the phonograph. It was the Beatles' album *Rubber Soul.* I had never heard the Beatles before. That's how long I was in the library.

"I want you to hear this one first," Vida said.

We sat there quietly listening to the record.

"Who sang that?" I said.

"John Lennon," she said.

Foster came back with the food and started cooking our dinnerbreakfast thing. Soon the whole attic was filled with the smell of onions.

That was months ago.

It's now the last of May and we're all living together in a little house in Berkeley. It has a small back yard. Vida's working at a topless place over in North Beach, so she'll have some money to go back to school next fall. She's going to give English another try. Foster has a girlfriend who is an exchange student from Pakistan. She's twenty and majoring in sociology.

She's in the other room now cooking up a big Pakistani dinner and Foster is watching her with a can of beer in his hand. He's got a job at Bethlehem Steel over in San Francisco at night working on an aircraft carrier that's in dry dock being fixed. Today is Foster's day off.

Vida is off doing something or other and will be home soon. She doesn't work tonight either. I've spent the afternoon at a table across from Sproul Hall where they took all those hundreds of Free

Speech kids off to jail in 1964. I've been gathering contributions for The American Forever, Etc.

I like to set my table up around lunch time near the fountain, so I can see the students when they come pouring through Sather Gate like the petals of a thousand-colored flowers. I love the joy of their intellectual perfume and the political rallies they hold at noon on the steps of Sproul Hall.

It's nice near the fountain with green trees all around and bricks and people that need me. There are even a lot of dogs that hang around the plaza. They are of all shapes and colors. I think it's important that you find things like this at the University of California.

Vida was right when she said that I would be a hero in Berkeley.